Praise for Melody Carlson's
Diary of a Teenage Girl, Caitlin Book 2:
It's My Life

"Melody has done it again! Teens won't be able to resist Caitlin's latest diary. Teens will identify and laugh with Caitlin and gain spiritual insight from this fresh glimpse into the heart of a very real teenage girl."

HEATHER KOPP, AUTHOR OF *LOVE STORIES GOD TOLD* AND
I STOLE GOD FROM GOODY TWO-SHOES

"This book inspired me to persevere through all my hardships and struggles, and it also brought me to the reality that even through my flaws, God can make Himself known in a powerful, life-changing way."

MEGHAN MCAULAY, 14-YEAR-OLD REVIEWER

"I definitely recommend *It's My Life* to teens. Even if you haven't read the first book, it's very easy to pick up what's going on. I was surprised at how easily I could relate my own life to Caitlin's. I really got involved with the book. I could hardly put it down!"

HEATHER SCHWARZBURG, 16-YEAR-OLD REVIEWER

"What an awesome way to convey what teenagers are faced with in today's world. *It's My Life* captures the expressions and feelings every teenager may face and the inner struggles they battle as they try to find a solution. A must-read not only for teens but adults too."

KORINA MOYER, YOUTH STAFF VOLUNTEER

Diary of a Teenage Girl, Caitlin Book 1:
Becoming Me

"From the first page, *Diary* captured me. I couldn't stop reading! This is a brilliant, well-crafted imaginary journey to the heart of a sixteen-year-old. I can't wait for the sequel!"

ROBIN JONES GUNN, BESTSELLING AUTHOR OF THE GLENBROOKE SERIES, THE CHRISTY MILLER SERIES, AND THE SIERRA JENSEN SERIES

"As I read *Diary*…I felt as if I had been given a gift—a 'backstage pass' into the life and heart of Caitlin O'Conner. It is a wonderful and mysterious ride as we are allowed a rare chance to travel alongside a teenage girl as she lives in the real

P9-BZR-349

world. This is a unique and refreshing read—fun and entertaining, while at the same time moving and insightful. Read and learn."

GEOFF MOORE, CONTEMPORARY CHRISTIAN RECORDING ARTIST

"Creative and impactful! *Diary* drew me in as my concern for Caitlin and her friends grew stronger each page I turned. It gave me the inside story to issues I see in my own life—and among my friends and peers. I recommend this book to every teenage girl going through the struggles of peer pressure, dating, and other temptations we face in life."

DANAE JACOBSON, 16-YEAR-OLD REVIEWER

"Melody Carlson writes with the clear, crisp voice of today's adolescent. *Diary of a Teenage Girl* is sure to please any teenager who is struggling with peer pressure, identity, and a desire to know and understand God's will. A moving, tender story that will be remembered…and loved."

ANGELA ELWELL HUNT, BESTSELLING AUTHOR OF *THE IMMORTAL* AND *MY LIFE AS A MIDDLE SCHOOL MOM*

"Melody Carlson captures the voice of teens today in a character we can all relate to. The unique peer perspective makes it very effective. Integrating the crucial message of the gospel, it forces us to weigh issues and causes us to look at a young person—in reality, ourselves—objectively. It challenges, convicts, and leaves us with hope for the future. I highly recommend this book."

ANGELA ALCORN, COLLEGE STUDENT, COAUTHOR OF *PRINCE ISHBANE'S LETTERS*, AND DAUGHTER OF RANDY ALCORN, BESTSELLING AUTHOR OF *DEADLINE, DOMINION,* AND *LORD FOULGRIN'S LETTERS*

"Carlson succeeds in weaving Christian beliefs into the plot with a light hand—and it's a darn good read!"

NAPRA REVIEW SERVICE

"As a teacher I found *Diary* to be a realistic look into the lives of Caitlin O'Conner and her friends. This book is dynamic, challenging, and fun!"

JAMI LYN WEBER, MOTHER AND FORMER HIGH SCHOOL TEACHER

DIARY OF A TEENAGE GIRL

CAITLIN BOOK N°. 2

IT'S MY LIFE

A NOVEL

MELODY CARLSON

Multnomah®Publishers *Sisters, Oregon*

IT'S MY LIFE
published by Multnomah Publishers, Inc.

and in association with the literary agency of Sara A. Fortenberry

© 2001 by Melody Carlson
International Standard Book Number: 1-59052-053-X

Cover design by David Carlson Design
Cover image by Getty Images/Karen Beard

Scripture quotations are from:
The Holy Bible, New International Version © 1973, 1984 by International Bible Society, used by permission of Zondervan Publishing House

Multnomah is a trademark of Multnomah Publishers, Inc., and is registered in the U.S. Patent and Trademark Office.
The colophon is a trademark of Multnomah Publishers, Inc.

Printed in the United States of America

For information:
MULTNOMAH PUBLISHERS, INC.•POST OFFICE BOX 1720•SISTERS, OREGON 97759

Library of Congress Cataloging-in-Publication Data
Carlson, Melody.
    It's my life by Caitlin O'Conner / by Melody Carlson.
       p.cm.
Summary: Sixteen-year-old Caitlin struggles with her feelings about her best friend's pregnancy, boys who tempt her to break her vow not to date, non-Christian friends, and what God may be calling her to do with her life.
    ISBN 1-57673-772-1 (pbk.)
    ISBN 1-59052-053-X
  [1. Christian life—Fiction. 2. Friendship—Fiction. 3. Conduct of life—Fiction. 4. Missionaries—Fiction. 5. Diaries—Fiction.] I. Title.
    PZ7.C216637 It 2001
    [Fic]—dc21

                                00-011386

05 06 07 08— 12 11 10 9

ONE

Friday, July 13 (I'm back...)

Is it just me or is this world going totally nuts?

Okay, before I get carried away, let me first say how good it feels to pick up a pen and write in my diary again. I thought I wanted to take a little break from writing in my diary during the summer—you know how it gets with work and sunshine and fun stuff to do. Anyway, I somehow imagined I was too busy to keep writing about my life. Big mistake, Caitlin! The thing is, I <u>need</u> to write about my life. Like, it sort of clears out my head or something— makes things more understandable. Almost like praying, but not quite the same.

Anyway, back to the world going totally nuts. Or is it me? You see, I've been working at my dad's advertising firm (actually I'm just a part-time receptionist, and not doing such a bad job if I do say so myself). But lately it seems like all these older guys have been hitting on me. Okay, now I know that sounds all narcissistic (a word I just read in a magazine, which means you think the whole world revolves around you, which I don't really think, by the way). But I don't think I'm imagining it either. I mean, Todd Alberts (who's probably at least twenty-five) even asked me if I wanted to go get coffee with him today. Now, it's not that I'm not flattered (because, believe me, I am!). But sheesh, I'm only sixteen (well, almost seventeen) for Pete's sake! But in Todd's defense, I doubt that he even knows my age, and he's probably just being friendly. And I'm sure if he knew I was still in high school he'd run the other way—and fast. But here's the honest truth—it feels pretty good to be noticed like that. And yet at the same time, it bugs me that it feels good. You know, like I should be above those sorts of feelings. Especially after making my vow to God about sex and dating. It's like I just wish those feelings (you know, feeling interested in a cute guy) would all just go away, once and for all. But they don't. So why is that?

Well, to make a long story short, I nicely told Todd thanks but no thanks (not in those exact words!). And now I feel kind of bad because he actually looked sort of hurt and disappointed. But maybe someone in the corporation will set him straight about me and how old guys like him shouldn't go around hitting on high school girls. Big laugh!

But now that I've vented over something pretty unimportant, let me get to what's really bugging me. It's Beanie Jacobs, my supposedly best friend. I say supposedly because lately she's been treating me like I've got smallpox or something. I mean, every single time I call her to invite her to go do something, she makes some totally lame excuse not to come. Okay, I know she's pregnant and not feeling too cool lately, but it's not like it's _my_ fault, and all I'm trying to do is to be the good friend that I've promised her I would be.

Like tonight, for instance, I just wanted someone to hang with. You know, go to the mall or something simple like that, and she says, "Sorry, I can't." Just like that. Not even an explanation, apology—nada, nothing. Well, instead of me grilling her like I usually do, I just said, "Well, fine!" and hung up—bam! Which, to tell the truth, left me feeling pretty rotten inside. Because I know she doesn't need that from me or anyone else right now.

But, I ask you, how far backwards is a person supposed to bend for her these days? I mean, it's not like she's a whole lot of fun to be with right now. And now she's all worried about putting on weight and getting fat, which, if you ask me, she should've considered before she got all hot and heavy with Zach last spring! Okay, there I go getting all preachy and judgmental again. And Beanie accuses me of doing that a lot lately. In fact, she even sarcastically calls me "Sister Caitlin" sometimes, which totally fries me!

So anyway, I called up Andrea LeMarsh, after being turned down by Beanie, and we went to the mall and hung out and had a really fun time (at least when I wasn't feeling guilty about Beanie). Andrea and I both got these totally cool Hawaiian print bikinis—and we imagined ourselves wearing them on some sandy beach in Mexico next month when the youth group goes on their missions trip. (Okay, I know we're primarily going there to help poor people and stuff, but we plan to have some fun along the way too!) But the whole time we've shopping and joking around and having a great time, I'm thinking how fun it would be if <u>Andrea</u> were my best friend instead of Beanie. And just thinking those kind of thoughts makes me feel really, really low. Because I <u>do</u> know that despite Beanie's prickly disposition of late, she really does love me, deep down, and she needs me too.

So, here's my struggle: Just because my best friend has totally messed up her life by getting pregnant, does this mean I must also sacrifice <u>my</u> summer, <u>my</u> fun, <u>my</u> life just to hang with her while she's being all depressed and glum and tired? I mean, I do believe in loyalty and I'd never stop loving Beanie or caring for her. But what I want to know is: Is it really <u>my</u> responsibility to see her through this whole pregnancy thing? Good grief, it lasts nine months (practically a lifetime in teen years!). And quite frankly, the idea of hanging with a girlfriend who's obviously starting to look pretty pregnant (not to mention how she never seems to care about her appearance any-more!) is starting to wear on me.

Well, now it's plain to see what a rotten, selfish, low-down (and yes, I'm sure, narcissistic) person I truly am. But isn't this my life too? Don't I have the right to do what I want? To hang with whomever I please? I mean, <u>it's my life!!!</u>

And yet, I know (deep down inside of me, someplace where I want to just plug my ears and cover my eyes sometimes) that this is definitely NOT what Jesus would do. I know, good and well, He would NOT treat His friends like that. Sheesh, He wouldn't even treat His enemies like that. And I can just imagine what Clay would say to me right now. In fact, I still vividly remember that time (just a couple weeks before he was shot and killed) when he told our youth group about how he wanted us to love one another like Jesus did, by putting each other above ourselves. And sure, it might sound nice and easy, but let me tell you, it's really not.

Oh, crud, I still have soooo much to learn about being a Christian.

DEAR GOD, IT SEEMS I'LL NEVER GET THIS RIGHT. ONE MINUTE I THINK I'M DOING PRETTY WELL, AND THE NEXT THING I KNOW I'M HAVING TOTALLY SELF-ISH AND SHALLOW THOUGHTS. HOW LONG WILL IT TAKE FOR ME TO REALLY CHANGE?

Saturday, July 14 (oh, brother!)

We had another car wash today (to earn more money for our Mexico trip). And naturally I didn't even bother to invite Beanie since she's made it perfectly clear that "no way, no how" is she going with us down to Mexico in August. Not that I blame her. I doubt I'd want to go either if I were in her shoes. So anyway, not wanting to bother Beanie, I called Andrea and then drove over and picked her up in my freshly washed car (no need to waste the youth group's time on it!), and we headed over to the minimall where we'd prearranged to hold the wash.

Well, last night Andrea and I both decided we'd try out our new bikinis today. (I mean, why shouldn't we enjoy them while it's hot and sunny and we're getting all wet anyway?) And to our pleasant surprise, they didn't hurt business at all. Man, you should have seen how many cars pulled over being driven by guys who obviously wanted to flirt. (We were halfway tempted to hose a couple of 'em down, but then we might've missed out on some tips.) So as you can imagine, it was a pretty successful fund-raiser. In fact, the best car wash event we've had so far this year.

But here's the clincher. After it's all said and done, Josh Miller (the guy who broke my heart last spring before I gave up dating completely) has recently joined our youth group and is now planning to go to Mexico with us. So anyway, he pulls Andrea and me aside like he's got something really important to tell us. So I'm thinking he's probably going to say something nice about how hard we worked and all, which makes sense due to the fact he's in charge of the car wash today (because Greg Thiessen, our regular youth group leader, had to be the best man at his brother's wedding).

So anyway, we cheerfully come over to listen, and then he says, "You girls think it's wise to be showing so much skin around here?" I mean, he just says this totally weird thing without even batting an eyelash.

Of course, I get all indignant and say, "Just what do you mean by that?"

Then he sort of shrugs and says, "Well, it just seems a little un-Christian to go around half naked like that."

Now that really makes me mad and I snap at him, "Sheesh, Josh, we've been working real hard here today, and we're just trying to be cool and comfortable, and all you can do is snipe at us!"

"Yeah, I know, Caitlin." He suddenly looks slightly uneasy, like maybe he wishes he'd never brought this ridiculous subject up. And for some reason his discomfort pleases me a little. (Okay, you already know I'm human!)

Then he says, "But you should really think about us guys. You know, we're supposed to be your brothers." Then he sort of laughs but not quite. "Maybe you sisters should have a little mercy on us."

"So, are you suggesting our appearance creates some kind of a temptation for you?" asks Andrea in what seems a fairly flirtatious way (although she's just like that sometimes, and I don't think she even totally realizes how she comes across).

"Maybe," says Josh, then he reaches over to me and flips the string tie that's keeping my bikini top on. "You know, I'd think you'd be especially uncomfortable with something like this, Catie. I mean, what with your commitment to sexual purity and all that stuff."

Well, I'm sure my eyes must've flashed some sort of very un-Christianlike message right then, but somehow I managed to answer in a rather quiet, albeit hostile, tone. "Since when does what I wear in any way reflect my personal beliefs or convictions?"

He shrugs again. "I don't know, Catie. It just seems to me you're sending out some pretty weird mixed messages." Then he walks away and starts coiling up the hoses.

Well, Andrea and I just stood there and laughed at him; then we took down the car wash signs, got into my car, and I drove off—fast. Because I was still irked. And all I could think was: The nerve of that guy! After all our hard work, all he could comment on was our unacceptable attire. Who does he think he is anyway, God's fashion police? I mean, grow up, Josh Miller! All of which I expressed to Andrea, but she just threw back her head and laughed. She hadn't taken one single word seriously. She just thought the whole thing was a joke.

But I really don't think Josh was joking. And to be completely honest, I must confess that he has actually got me to thinking about what he said. And I'm wondering if he might not be partially right about me sending those "mixed messages." (Although I refuse to admit as much to him just yet.) And at the same time I still wonder, what right does he have to judge me in the first place?

I mean, is he trying to imply that just because I made a promise to God to remain sexually pure, that I should go around dressed like a nun or something? How fair is that? Why shouldn't I dress however I want? Last time I checked it was still my life. And if he's got a problem

with my appearance, he can just look the other way!
Can't he? Or maybe not. I'm not entirely sure anymore.
But I guess I will consider what he said, and I'll try not to
be too mad at him for saying it. I suppose he was just trying to be honest, even if he was pretty irritating and
judgmental about it. And maybe I'll even ask Greg about
all this tomorrow in youth group. Or maybe not.

Well, I do know this, I will ask God about it. Because,
it's like Clay used to say—convictions are a personal
thing—they need to come straight from God and
directly to you—no middleman needed.

DEAR GOD, SHOW ME WHAT YOU WANT ME TO DO
ABOUT THINGS LIKE STRING BIKINIS AND THE LIKE.
AND SHOW ME HOW YOU WANT ME TO LIVE. AND
THEN HELP ME TO BE WILLING TO OBEY. AMEN.

two

Sunday, July 15 (a little ranting)

As usual, I saved Beanie a seat next to me in youth group today. But when she came in, Andrea and I were in the middle of an intense conversation and so it might have appeared that I was ignoring Beanie, but I wasn't. Not consciously anyway.

Naturally, Beanie took offense (Aunt Steph says it has to do with her hormones being all mixed up right now), but she huffed off and sat all by herself in the back of the room. And <u>that</u> made me mad. I didn't see why she had to act that way. So after youth group, when she stormed off without even saying hi, I never even went to look for her. I figured if she wants to act like a child, I'd just let her. She'll have to grow up soon enough as it is. Which brings me to another weird thing that I've been trying not to think about. Lately, Beanie has been talking like she might actually keep her baby. I think that some-how, probably from baby-sitting little Oliver or something, Beanie's gotten this crazy idea that she'd make a good mom. Now, I'm not saying she wouldn't, but why in the world would anyone in her right mind want to be stuck with taking care of a baby when she's only seventeen???

So, for me to say that Beanie and I haven't been exactly seeing things eye to eye lately is a gross under-statement. If you ask me, I think she's living in another universe, like Baby La La Land or Barney World or some-thing. I mean, who does she think is going to support her and her baby? Certainly not her mom, Lynn, who hasn't called her once since Beanie moved out. And I've even heard that the government doesn't have too many wel-fare funds available for single moms these days. And this brings me to another sore subject. Zach. Now talk about an amazing disappearing act—you'd think he'd moved to another planet. But no, he still lives in town and still works for the parks, last I heard. And I'm sure he still plans on using his athletic scholarship to go to college, where he'll probably forget all about this baby business. But do we ever see him at youth group anymore? No! Does he ever call Beanie? Think again! Arggh! It just makes me so furious, I can hardly even write his name in my diary without tearing through the paper.

But while I'm ranting, let me say this—it takes two to make a baby. And, without a doubt, Beanie has done her part. (Although she's admitted to me that doing "it" really wasn't that much fun.) But it seems totally unfair that she now has to bear this thing alone! But that's what she's determined to do. She says Zach's only solu-tion to her pregnancy (despite that "great" talk he had with Pastor Tony) is still abortion. And according to Beanie, he wants nothing to do with her or the child he's fathered unless she agrees to "terminate the preg- nancy" (his terminology <u>not</u> mine!). And what totally sends me is that I used to really admire that guy. Now I think he's nothing but a great big hypocrite, not to mention a totally selfish jerk!

But Jesus says we're supposed to love, not just our friends, but our enemies as well. Grrrr! And I think the Bible says we're even supposed to <u>pray</u> for them! Well, I'll need some serious help to honestly love Zach, but I guess I can try to pray for him—maybe then God will knock some sense into the stupid blockhead!

DEAR GOD, HELP ME TO LOVE ZACH (BECAUSE RIGHT NOW I REALLY CAN'T STAND TO EVEN THINK OF HIM). AND PLEASE SHOW HIM WHAT YOU THINK ABOUT ALL THIS, AND PLEASE HELP HIM TO MAKE THE KIND OF DECISIONS THAT HONOR YOU. AND COULD YOU ALSO PLEASE SHOW ME HOW I CAN BE A BETTER FRIEND TO BEANIE—I KNOW SHE NEEDS ME, BUT WHY DOES SHE KEEP PUSHING ME AWAY?

Wednesday, July 18 (happy birthday to me!)

Yipeeee!!! I am now officially seventeen. You know, it's hard having one of those "late birthdays"—I mean, all your friends get to turn a year older during the school year, and you're just left behind. As a result, birthdays have always been sort of a big deal to me.

And the day started out nice enough, with my family singing to me and Mom bringing me breakfast in bed. (Okay, it was just Cheerios, but she did put a flower on the tray.) But even my younger brother, Ben, was up (no small miracle), and my parents gave me a sweet card with a big, fat check to be used toward my Mexico trip! And then Mom had gotten me this very cool jacket that I'd admired in a catalog a couple weeks ago.

Then some of the ladies at work threw a little party for me at break time (with a sweet little cake and several balloons). Of course, as a result, the word quickly circulated that "Caitlin, the receptionist, is only seventeen!" And I saw some surprised looks on some of the faces (like Todd Alberts's, for instance). But I just laughed it off. I don't mind when people think I'm older, but it's a relief having the truth out (not that I'd been hiding anything from anybody).

All in all, I thought I was having a pretty good day, but then after dinner my dad talked me into going with him to get some ice cream to go with Mom's scrumptious chocolate-sour cream cake. And when we got back, I couldn't help but notice several extra cars parked around my house—and low and behold, the parents had planned a little surprise party for me. Mostly friends, family, and people from church. But it was nice.

Beanie came with Aunt Steph (who I noticed spent most of the evening talking with Pastor Tony). But I realized this was the first time Beanie had been at my house (when my parents were both there) since they'd heard about her pregnancy. And suddenly I realized how she was probably still uncomfortable with this whole thing. Unfortunately, it seemed my parents were too. They both treated her sort of stiff and formal, kind of like, "Good to see you, Beanie. Hope you're feeling well these days." No joking around or anything. It made me feel pretty bad for her. I'll have to ask them to loosen up for Beanie's sake. She feels lousy enough about her "mistake" without them getting all weirded out on her too.

Which reminds me of another thing. My parents and I have never really discussed this whole thing very much (I mean Beanie's pregnancy). And I'm positive they have no idea, right now, that she might actually <u>keep</u> the baby. I'm sure they don't quite know what to think about this whole thing as it is, but I can't imagine what they'd say about my best friend being a teenage mom. Probably that's why we haven't really spoken of it. Maybe it's all for the best.

And one more thing before I call it a night. Josh came tonight too. No big surprise there, since he's pretty involved with our youth group these days. But he'd given Andrea a ride. And I hate to admit it, but that bothered me. Now, I'm not exactly sure which bothered me more: the fact that Josh (the boy I used to swoon over) gave Andrea a ride, or that Andrea (my almost best friend) got a ride with Josh. And I'm sure that doesn't even make sense in writing. But I'm pretty sure it has to do with jealousy, I'm just not sure why. Well, sometimes life's just too complicated to figure it all out. And besides it's like _my_ birthday, and hey, why should I even care?

But for some mysterious reason I do. So, let me go on just a little here, if I may. Just as the party is winding down, Josh takes me aside and rather sweetly wishes me a happy birthday, and for a split second I almost think he's going to kiss me (and I can't even begin to sift through what I think about _that!_), but then he _doesn't_. Instead, he just looks into my eyes and tells me how much he loves me "_as a sister_," and then he says he's sorry for that stuff he said at the car wash last weekend, and that he was probably out of line for talking to me like that. Well, I just blink and say, "That's okay. I've forgotten all about it." Which is almost true. I _almost_ had forgotten it.

But for some reason the whole incident left me feeling a little unsettled inside, and I'm wondering: Did I want him to kiss me? Which seems totally stupid. And then when I saw Josh and Andrea getting into his little Jeep Wrangler, something inside me just twisted, sort of. And so I plan to spend some time praying about all this before I go to bed tonight. I really would like to understand what's going on here. If that's even possible. If not, maybe I can just pray to forget the whole thing. Because if there's one thing I've learned this year—the heart is a fickle thing.

DEAR GOD, WHY CAN'T SOMETHING LIKE GIVING UP
BOYS AND DATING JUST BE EASY? YOU SAY IT, YOU

DO IT, IT'S DONE. FINISHED. BUT IT'S JUST NOT THAT SIMPLE, IS IT? I NEED YOUR HELP TO LIVE THIS LIFE YOU'VE LAID BEFORE ME, GOD. I FEEL LIKE UNDERNEATH THIS SMOOTH EXTERIOR OF "CAITLIN SURE HAS IT ALL TOGETHER" I'M JUST A GREAT BIG MESS THAT'S FALLING APART FAST. I KNOW HOW I COULD EASILY BE IN BEANIE'S SHOES RIGHT NOW, OR EVEN IN THE FUTURE, IF I'M NOT CAREFUL. SO PLEEEEASE, GOD, HELP ME TO HONOR MY PROMISE TO YOU. PLEASE GIVE ME YOUR STRENGTH AND YOUR WISDOM TO FOLLOW YOU WITH EVERYTHING I'VE GOT. I JUST CAN'T SEE ANY OTHER WAY TO DO THIS THING. AMEN!

Thursday, July 19 (whose life is this anyway?)

Okay, I'm putting in a hard week at work. I even chauffeur my little brother and three of his buds to a baseball game this evening so my parents can go out. I'm living a responsible and mature sort of life, but then I want to go and spend the weekend with my friend, and my parents come totally unglued. What is it with parents anyway? They want you to act like an adult, but then they refuse to treat you like one.

"This is so sudden," says my mom. "We don't even know Andrea's father." As if the man might be an ax murderer or child molester or something equally despicable. You see, Andrea's parents are divorced; her mom's remarried to a nice guy, and her dad's still single. But he has a girl-friend (or two, according to Andrea, which I did not tell my parents—no need to add fuel to their little fire). Anyway, her dad has this really cool cabin on a lake with a dock and a ski boat and everything. And he invited Andrea to come up this weekend and to bring along a friend, and she called me.

"How do we know who's going to be up there?" asks my dad suspiciously.

"Who do you think will be up there?" I toss back.

"He might have friends. You know, it might be a party weekend, with who knows what going on—"

"Why would a dad invite his daughter and her friend if he wanted to party, as you put it? I mean, think about it, Dad. Is that what you would do?" Thankfully, this seems to fluster him a little. And it's not that I want to be disrespectful exactly. I mean, really, I don't. But I want to go, and spending the weekend at the lake sounds so great!

"But what if something happens? You say there's no phone," says my ever-practical mother.

"If you're that worried, you could just let me take your cell phone," I wisely counter. "Really, Mom and Dad, I've been trying to show you how mature I can be and now you're treating me like a baby." I eye Benjamin who, like a dog, is licking the remains of death-by-chocolate ice cream from his bowl. And to my surprise, this kid actually speaks up in my defense, probably trying to show some appreciation for me driving him and his friends around, which he should considering how Ryan Bender spilled a whole bag of popcorn all over the backseat of my car.

"Yeah, you guys should lighten up on Cate," he says as cool as can be, not realizing he has a brown smudge of ice cream on the tip of his nose. "She's been a good ol' gal lately."

My dad laughs at this, but then seems to consider the advice of this little male pubescent. "Yeah, maybe you're right, bud. Maybe we should let up on the ol' gal."

And I bite my tongue, waiting for the consensus.

"But what about—" my mom starts but thankfully never finishes.

"She can take my cell phone," offers my dad, taking control of the decision. "She's got her own car, and if for some reason something doesn't seem right, I'm sure she'll just phone us, climb in her car, and come straight home. Right, Catie?"

"Of course," I assure them. "It's not like I'm stupid or looking for trouble. And just for the record, I'm not the least bit worried. Besides, you've met Andrea's mom. Does she seem the sort of woman who would send her daughter and friend off into some bad situation?"

"I guess not." My mom seems slightly more at ease now. "It's just that we love you, sweetie." Then we all hug, and it's settled. Cool, I get to go!

But what bugs me is that we had to go through such turmoil just to get here. I don't see why they can't just trust my judgment about these things. I mean, some kids my age are already living out on their own. And I've been being all responsible and working and everything. So why are they so paranoid all the time? Good grief, this is _my_ life! I sure don't want to mess it up. Don't they realize that?

Okay, no more time for ranting. Right now I need to pack. We're leaving right after I finish work tomorrow, and the forecast is for hot, hot, hot. Ahh, to take a dip in a cool, mountain lake. Look out, fun times ahead!!!

THREE

Sunday, July 22 *(not what I expected)*

Man, am I glad to be home. Not that I didn't have fun. Well, mostly, anyway. But Andrea's dad isn't the most mature adult I've ever met. And his girlfriend is a real piece of work too. In a way they both remind me of a couple of high school kids who haven't grown up yet. Maybe they never will. I felt pretty bad for Andrea a couple times. But I assured her I didn't hold her responsible for their behavior.

Just the same we stuck it out. I know I probably should've come home sooner. But I honestly didn't feel like I was in any real danger. And I just couldn't bear to hear my parents say "I told you so," which I know they'd <u>think</u> even if they didn't say the actual words. Someday I'll tell them they were partially right. Just not yet.

Well, Andrea's dad, or Bobby, as he insisted I call him, has a pretty nice place at the lake, even if it was a total mess. And Jeanie (his girlfriend who looks just like a middle-aged cocktail waitress, which she is by the way) doesn't lift a finger to help out. So to start with, Andrea and I spent our first evening there cleaning house and doing laundry so we could have clean sheets, then we made a run to the nearby camp store where I paid $76.83 for two small bags of groceries!!! Then we proceeded to cook dinner for _everyone_. All the while, Bobby and Jeanie were just hanging around like a couple of overgrown kids, and never once offered to help. Too weird.

I thought maybe things would change by the next day. I mean, which ones were supposed to be the guests here? But nothing changed. Andrea and I fixed breakfast and cleaned up again. Then Andrea talked Bobby into dragging us around the lake in the ski boat, but by noon he'd consumed so much beer that we decided we'd be safer to get him and the boat to dockside. Then we took out the canoe by ourselves (which was really pretty fun). But when we returned by midafternoon, Jeanie's younger sister and her boyfriend had just shown up. But did they offer to help or bring any food or anything? (Yeah, sure, you bet.) Nope, they were just a couple of freeloaders. Well, Andrea and I were getting kind of ticked by then. So we got ourselves all cleaned up, then sneaked out the back door, got in my car, and drove to the nearby town for pizza.

Now _that_ was fun! A couple of local boys began flirting with us, and at first we tried to ignore them, but then, being all inspired by our maturity, we decided we'd use this opportunity to tell them about Jesus (thinking that would either send the guys packing or perhaps do the kingdom some good!). And can you believe it? They listened—eagerly. We told them all about how our dear friend, Clay Berringer, had been shot last spring (and of course, they'd read about it in the papers), and we told them about the impact this whole thing had had on us. And they were sincerely interested. And when we finally left, they thanked us for telling them all that stuff. <u>Unbelievable</u>! Andrea and I were on such a complete high as I drove us back to her dad's cabin.

But it evaporated as soon as we got back, because when we walked in the front door, the place just reeked with pot smoke. That's when Andrea went totally ballistic. She just tore into her dad and his friends, telling them how irresponsible they all were and how she was completely sick of them. Then we went into our room and locked the door. It's not that we were afraid. Good grief, the four of them were so spaced out that her words probably went right over their dopey heads. But I guess we just wanted to separate ourselves from them. After that, we sat down on the bed and Andrea just burst into tears. She felt so humiliated by her dad's behavior. But I assured her it didn't matter to me. "He made those choices, not you," I said. "And it's not a reflection on you."

"But I feel so stupid," she said, wiping her tears with a beach towel.

"Look, if it makes you feel any better, I can tell you all sorts of horror stories about things I've been through with Beanie and her mom over the years—I mean, Lynn Jacobs is a whole lot more messed up than your dad. So don't worry, this stuff is nothing new to me." And fortunately that seemed to make her feel a little better.

Then I did something I don't usually do (but perhaps our chat with those local boys had emboldened me a little). "Do you want us to pray for your dad?" I offered, feeling a little self-conscious once the words were out.

At first, she got a real curious look on her face, but then she nodded. "Yes. Let's do that."

And so we did. We even prayed for Jeanie and her sister and her sister's boyfriend, and we prayed for those two local boys as well. Then, totally exhausted and not wanting to leave our room, we just visited a little while, then fell asleep.

And the next morning we got up early, got dressed, then slipped out quietly and went back to town where we attended the service in a church we'd noticed the night before. It was nothing like our regular church, just a lot of old people, but they seemed genuinely glad to have us there with them. Then we ate lunch at a little deli in town, went back to the cabin for another swim and a row around the lake, then told everyone good-bye and even thank you, and headed back home. So all in all, it wasn't such a bad weekend. Still, I'm not ready to tell my parents all the details yet.

DEAR GOD, THANK YOU FOR SHOWING ME THAT MY PARENTS MAY HAVE SOME DISCERNMENT AFTER ALL. AND HELP ME TO RESPECT THEM MORE. (ACTUALLY, AFTER THE LAST COUPLE DAYS, I REALLY DO!!!) BUT BY THE SAME TOKEN, I THANK

YOU FOR TAKING WHAT COULD HAVE BEEN A
REALLY CRUDDY SITUATION AND MAKING IT
BETTER. AMEN.

Tuesday, July 24 (Beanie's baby)

It's very late, but I must get all this down before I col-
lapse in bed. I got the call from Aunt Steph late this
afternoon. Her voice was breathless as she quickly
explained. "Cate, there's been an accident. It's Beanie.
She's in the ER right now. Can you come?" I quickly got
one of the office ladies to take over the switchboard
and tried not to speed to the hospital, which is, thankfully, just a few blocks away. Holding back tears and
waves of panic, I raced across the parking lot, praying for
Beanie with each step. What had happened to her? Was
she going to be okay?

I found Steph and Mom standing in the ER waiting
room and through bits and pieces they both told me
what had happened.

"She took Oliver to the park, just like she often does,"
began Steph. "He's okay. He's with Ben right now. But he
was in his stroller and you know how he's just figured out
how to undo everything. Apparently he undid the seat
belt." Then Steph began to cry.

"It seems he got out while Beanie wasn't looking," continued Mom. "And she saw him heading straight for the
street, and a car was coming—"

"And the driver said that Beanie shoved him out of

the way just in time, but she got hit!" sobbed Steph, her voice shaking. "Beanie actually risked her own life for my baby!"

I grabbed Steph's arms, tears now tumbling down my cheeks too. "But is she okay? Is Beanie okay? Please, tell me!"

"We don't know."

And for the longest time, we didn't know. We waited and waited for what seemed like years. And finally, at about seven o'clock, the nurse said Beanie had been stabilized and was being moved to a private room for the night, and that one of us could go visit her shortly. After a brief discussion, Mom and Steph both decided that, as her best friend, I should go. And so I went in to see Beanie. Her head was bandaged and a tube came out of her arm, but she was awake and her eyes, though sad, were fairly clear. "Beanie?" I whispered as I gently touched her bruised hand. "Are you okay?"

"I'm alive," she said in a raspy voice.

"I'm so thankful. I've really been praying. I couldn't stand to lose you, Beanie. I've just been realizing how important your friendship is to me." I started crying all over again. But I didn't care. I was just so glad to see she was okay. "How do you feel?"

"I've felt better."

I smiled. Same old Beanie. "But did you break any- thing?"

"A couple ribs, and a concussion." Then she began to cry, silently, but the tears were flowing down her cheeks in two steady streams, and I could see she was in bad pain.

"Are you okay?"

"I lost my baby." She choked on the words.

I just stared at her, not knowing what to say. I was sad for her, but to be perfectly honest, part of me was relieved. And even as I write these words, I know it's so very wrong of me (PLEASE FORGIVE ME, GOD!), but I actually thought, at least this is one less thing for Beanie to bear. But somehow (THANK GOD!) I knew that wasn't what she needed to hear. "I'm so sorry," was all I said, and then I carefully put my arms around her, not wanting to hurt her further, and then we both cried together for what seemed a pretty long time.

I pulled up a chair and just listened as she talked about all the things she wouldn't get to do with her baby. Once again, I must be honest and say I really didn't understand much of what she was saying, and I'd had no idea she was looking forward to having a child like that. And I just kept thinking this whole thing was a real blessing in disguise. But believe me, I NEVER said it. Not even once. I just listened and nodded and told her everything was going to be okay, that it'd get better, and that she'd get over this in time.

I could tell by the commotion in the hallway that Lynn Jacobs was here and she was demanding to see her daughter immediately. I could hear Steph trying to reason with her, but finally it was of no use and Lynn just burst right into Beanie's room. I stayed in the chair, positioning myself between Lynn and Beanie, determined to lay down my life if necessary to protect Beanie from Lynn's wrath. But I couldn't protect her from her mother's cruel and heartless words.

"I just learned from the doctor that you lost <u>your baby</u>!" Lynn exploded. "What I want to know is <u>what baby</u>? What the ----- is going on with you, Sabrina Jacobs? You went and got yourself knocked up and then you didn't even tell your own mother—" Thankfully that was when a strong orderly (I later learned he was accosted by an angry Aunt Stephie) came in and literally dragged Lynn out of the room, loudly warning her that they could have the police there within minutes. Then Steph came in and comforted Beanie. I was so glad to hear Steph soothing Beanie, saying all those important things that I could never have thought of.

Anyway, we stayed there until really late. Until Beanie finally seemed to be calmed down and able to sleep. The nurses even posted a guard by Beanie's door, promising that Lynn Jacobs was now restricted from the hospital.

And so here I am. It's almost 2 A.M. and I'm exhausted, but fear I will not be able to sleep. So much to take in. So much sadness in Beanie's life. So much guilt in me for not being a better, more understanding friend. How could I have ever turned my back on Beanie? Not that I really did (well, not recently anyway), but I'd been thinking about it. And just because she was pregnant. Good grief! Sometimes I just really make myself sick!

DEAR GOD, PLEASE, PLEASE FORGIVE ME. I AM SO
SORRY. PLEASE, PLEASE FORGIVE ME—AGAIN AND
AGAIN AND AGAIN AND AGAIN AND...

FOUR

Wednesday, July 25 (hard stuff)

I went to see Beanie after work today. She's out of the hospital and back at Steph's now. Apparently the most serious thing about the accident was losing the baby. I didn't really know that at the time, but that's what Steph says.

Anyway, Beanie was really, really down tonight. Talk about the blues.... Steph says (once again) that it's probably just hormones playing havoc with Beanie's heart (she calls it the "baby blues"), but I think it's more than that. I mean, when I consider all the pain Beanie's endured in her seventeen years, I can hardly believe she's survived it at all. I'm pretty sure it would have killed a wimp like me. All I can say is that Beanie must be made out of some pretty strong stuff. I just hope it's strong enough. But I'm praying for her like never before. And even though she told me she's mad at God now, I feel pretty sure she'll get over it. In time. At least, I hope so.

In the meantime, Steph says she needs lots of TLC, and that's just what we're going to give her. Even my mom

is stepping up to the plate. She and Ben will help watch
Oliver and Beanie during the daytime. And I'll go over
and spend time with her in the evenings. And hopefully
between all of us, Beanie will see that she's loved—and
that she has family. I told her that even if we're not bio-
logically related, we're all related by God, and I think
that's what matters most in the long run anyway.

But when I left Steph's apartment tonight, Beanie's
eyes looked so flat to me. Sort of glazed over with pain, I
guess. It's hard to explain, but it's like her old spark is
totally gone. She almost seems dead to me. I know that
sounds absolutely horrible and morbid and I don't mean it
as a judgment against her. More like an observation
about her. But it just makes me so sad. Sadder than I
can even describe with words. Oh, poor, poor Beanie.

DEAR GOD, PLEASE, I BEG YOU, BREATHE YOUR
LIFE BACK INTO MY SISTER BEANIE. PLEASE SHOW
HER HOW MUCH YOU LOVE HER. PLEASE, PLEASE
WRAP YOUR ARMS AROUND HER, AND PLEASE HOLD
HER SAFELY IN YOUR HANDS. AMEN.

Friday, July 27 (a faint ray of hope)

For the first time since Beanie lost her baby, she seemed
to show a flicker of interest in life tonight. Okay, maybe
it was because of the pizza and the video that I
brought over—but hey, whatever it takes, right?

Anyway, Steph and Tony were taking Oliver to a kiddy

carnival at another church tonight. They said it was to get ideas for a fall carnival at our church, although I suspect this might just be a thinly veiled disguise for an actual _date_. (Which is perfectly all right by me—I mean, sheesh, I've never said that _everyone_ on the planet should give up dating altogether). Furthermore I happen to think Tony and Steph make a really great couple and I'd love to see them actually tie the knot someday. Although Steph firmly tells me they are only "good friends." Well, to that I say: Time will tell.

But back to Beanie. I wanted to do something special for her, to hopefully lift her spirits out of the deep, dark dungeon she's been inhabiting of late. So, I rented one of her all-time favorite "feel good" movies (_Ever After_— where Drew Barrymore plays this no-nonsense Cinderella chick, who actually sort of reminds me of Beanie), and we watched the movie while we ate pepperoni pizza with double cheese and consumed about two liters of Dr. Pepper. But I think I saw her actually smile a couple times.

But when it was all over she just sort of groaned and said, "Life sure isn't like the movies, is it?"

And trying to be funny, I said, "Oh, I don't know, sometimes life is like one of those really _bad_ movies." But I knew exactly what she meant. She meant: Life sure isn't a fairy tale, is it? No magical happy endings for me. So then I added, "But, you know, I _do_ believe with God in our lives we really can live happily ever after—if that's what you're thinking." Then she just rolled her eyes at me and said she still wasn't speaking to God. So I asked her why.

"Why?" she practically screams at me. "You're asking ME why? Good night, Cate, just look at my life. If this is the best God can do, I might as well go out and shoot myself."

Then I just kind of blinked at her and wondered how to respond to that. I mean, I sure didn't want to pull her down any farther, but I'm thinking—you're blaming God for the mess you made of your life? But, thank God, I did not say that. If I had, I'm pretty sure she would've gone off looking for a gun right then (which Steph doesn't keep by the way!). So I just stayed quiet for a moment, then I calmly said, "All I know is that God does love you, Beanie. And I'm sure He feels just as bad as you do about losing that baby. But at least your baby is up there safe with God right now."

And then she just started to cry again, and I was thinking: Great, now I've really gone and done it. But somehow her crying this time seemed different. It didn't seem quite like that hopeless, pitiful, just-jump-off-a-cliff sort of crying that I'd heard on and off all week long. This seemed more like a giving-up sort of crying. Like, maybe she was just surrendering all of this crummy, impossible-to-understand stuff to God. Anyway, I sure hope that's what it was. And that's what I'm praying for tonight.

So, then we hugged and I could tell she was really tired, so I told her to go to bed and get some rest and then I came home. Big sigh. This has been a pretty tough week for me (and everyone else too). But tonight I

glanced back over my diary and was embarrassingly
reminded of how I was whining and complaining about
wanting to have more fun last week. Well, I haven't even
considered "fun" this week. All I can think about is how
much we need God to get through this thing called <u>life</u>.
'Cuz it sure ain't easy! And right now I just want Beanie to
grab hold of God (like she'd been doing just a month or so
ago) and then just never, ever let go of Him. Because I
just don't think she (or I) can make it without Him.

DEAR GOD, PLEASE HELP US TO HANG ON TO YOU
FOR ALL THAT WE'RE WORTH. AND HELP US TO
NEVER, EVER LET GO. AMEN.

Sunday, July 29 (two weeks until Mexico!)

To my pleased surprise, Beanie came to church and
youth group today. And she really seems better. Almost
like her old self. <u>Almost</u>. And afterwards she came up
and hugged me and thanked me for sticking with her
through everything—and I could tell she really meant it.

Then she and I and Andrea went to the mall and
acted like real teenage girls for a pleasant change. And
I think Beanie enjoyed that. I'm sure it's the first time
she's acted like a "normal" seventeen-year-old girl for
months now. She's still a little sore from the accident
and she has this ugly yellowish purple splotch on her forehead. But other than that, to look at her, you almost
wouldn't know all that she's been through.

I'd already told Andrea the whole Beanie story (in fact, everyone at church knows because Tony put her on the prayer chain earlier this week), and today Andrea was really sweet and kind to Beanie. Then after I dropped Andrea home, I brought Beanie over to my house and she stayed for dinner, and my family was also really nice to her. And she even started making some of her old jokes to Ben (strangely enough, those two actually get along really well!). Anyway, it seemed like she was trying to get it back together.

Then we went up to my room to listen to a new Geoff Moore CD I bought at the mall today (our youth group leader was talking about the lyrics in a song of his). And that's when Beanie really opened up about all the stuff that had gone on between her and Zach. Like the way he'd sought her out at the beginning, and how he'd been the one to push their relationship along to new levels (and last spring I had thought it was her!). Even how he'd pressured her to have sex. Okay, in all fairness, I must admit this might've been the way I was hearing what she was saying, and I suppose she might really have been saying it differently. But just the same, it was all I could do not to jump up and freak out about what a total jerk I thought he was. But I knew that would only upset her, and I could see she just needed to talk. And also, underneath everything she was saying (and despite what an absolute moron he is), I suspect she still cares for him deeply. Don't ask me why. Because I can't, for the life of me, come up with one single good reason. But I'm pretty sure she does.

Anyway, she told me in detail about <u>everything</u> she'd gone through in the past several months. (And let me tell you, it hasn't exactly been a walk through the mall!) But the hardest part for her was the way Zach had treated her after she told him she was pregnant. Now I (for one) had always thought she'd played down how badly she'd been hurt by him then, but I had no idea just how totally crushed and devastated she'd actually been by their breakup. She even told me how she'd considered suicide numerous times—had actually planned it all out, step by step, written the notes and everything!

"But each time," she explained, "<u>something</u> would get in the way. Like a phone call, or a neighbor stopping by, just all sorts of things. And now I'm pretty sure that was God trying to protect me from myself."

"Good thing too." I reached over and put my hand on her shoulder. "You wouldn't consider doing anything like that now, would you? I mean, I realize you've been pretty down and everything lately."

"I don't think so." She looked directly at me, and her dark eyes still looked so sad, especially with the effects of her recent head injury shadowed beneath them. "But I guess you can never tell about these things, Cate. But I really don't think I <u>want</u> to die now. I think I <u>want</u> to live. I can feel this tiny little ember of hope burning inside of me. And I think it's God."

I nodded eagerly, holding back tears. "I <u>know</u> it is. And Beanie, I keep wanting to tell you something, but I'm afraid it'll sound so totally stupid."

"What is it? I'm sure you can't tell me anything that's any more stupid than I've been lately."

"I just want to tell you that I think you're one of the bravest people I know. And if I'd gone through everything you've gone through, I'm sure I wouldn't even be here. I'd probably be dead, for sure, or else locked up in some rubber cell somewhere. You are an incredibly strong person, Beanie. But even so, I _know_ you still need God just as much as I do."

"Yeah. I've been realizing that too."

So then I asked her a really tough question. I asked if she felt she'd totally given up Zach—or if she'd go back with him if he wanted to. And I must confess, I don't even know what the right answer would be—or even if there _is_ a right answer. I just wanted to know where she stood as far as Zach was concerned. Because in my book, right now, he's lower than slug slime. And if I ever see him, I'm afraid I'll have to tell him so.

"I don't really know, Cate. Right now, I do feel like I _can_ live without him. But to be honest, there was a time when I thought I couldn't. And I know it sounds so totally lame to say that. That's why I never told you before. I knew it sounded all sappy and sweet and not like something I'd ever fall into. But I did. Oh, man, I did. And I fell hard."

"Well, it wasn't all your fault. I think Zach gently nudged you over the edge when you fell."

She smiled a little at that. "Yeah, I suppose. But I was willing and eager. And when he told me how much he loved me, how he had never loved anyone the way he loved me, and how he would never love anyone as much, well, I just swallowed every line like it was the gospel truth." She looked me in the eyes. "But you know, it's because I wanted to believe it. Because I needed someone to love me like that. I'd never been loved like—" Then her voice broke again.

"God loves you like that," I said, instantly hoping she wouldn't call me "Sister Caitlin" again.

"I think I know that now."

"But I do understand what you're saying, Beanie. And I think someday you're going to have a love that's even better than what you had with Zach. And who knows, maybe it'll even be <u>with</u> Zach." (And I didn't even say that I sure hoped not!) "But I do believe some really cool Christian guy is going to come along someday. Maybe not for a while yet because you and I need to graduate high school and go to college and get that apartment we've always talked about first. But when it's the right time, your prince is going to come along, Beanie, and mark my word, you'll get married and you will live happily ever after. I just know it."

She smiled and shook her head with that old Beanie skepticism. "Well, as usual, you've got an excellent imagination, Cate. And who knows, you could even be right, but I guess, for the time being, I won't think about all that stuff. I'll just try to enjoy what I have right now."

And that's when I got my idea. But I knew I couldn't tell anyone just yet.

FIVE

Monday, July 30 (my big idea)

I prayed about this and got this really strong
sense of peace, like it's something I was supposed to do.
But just to be safe, I decided to check with my parents
and run it past Pastor Tony first.

You see, I really want for Beanie to be able to come
with us to Mexico. And I know she doesn't have much
money and really needs what she's managed to save.
Especially since her dear, sweet mother, Lynn, has pretty
much written her off. Big surprise there. But anyway, I
thought to myself: What if Beanie got some sort of anonymous missions scholarship or something? Because I know she
has way too much pride to allow someone else to pay her
way. But maybe if she didn't know who it was or exactly
why. Well, just maybe she would be able to accept it and
go. And I really think she _needs_ to go. I think it might help
her to heal and get back to being a "normal" teenager
again (if that's even possible).

So I checked with my parents and Pastor Tony and
they all thought it was a great idea, and actually

offered to chip in too. And we all promised to keep it top secret. Pastor Tony will present the gift to Beanie, just saying that an anonymous donor gave it, and then we'll all act real surprised and everything. I made sure even Ben didn't hear us talking. He's a good kid and all, but he can be a real blabbermouth sometimes.

Tony's going to give it to her tomorrow, and I just have to wait for the call and then act all surprised. This is fun!

Tuesday, July 31 (this isn't fun)

Okay, Beanie calls me up tonight, but she sounds kind of glum again. And then she tells me about how Pastor Tony just gave her this scholarship to go to Mexico and how she's not at all happy about it.

"But why not?" I ask, trying not to reveal anything. "I think it would be great if you came. We'd have so much fun together. What exactly is the problem anyway?"

"I just don't like taking charity."

"Beanie." I try to make my voice sound all serious and mature. "First of all, how do you know that someone in the church didn't hear God telling them to give it to you? I mean, you could in essence be saying no to God. And plus this trip is to help others who are less fortunate than you. Maybe the person who gave the scholarship can't go and they think if they send someone in their place, it will allow them to bless somebody else in Mexico. I mean, think about it, do you seriously want to be responsible for some poor Mexican kid losing this blessing?"

She kind of laughed at that. Then she said something that left me speechless. "You might be right, Cate. And now that I think about it, I wonder if Zach might've possibly donated this. You know, 'cause he feels so bad about everything and all. Maybe it's his way to make amends or something."

Well, my stomach just turned over, and I had to swallow hard to control myself from saying something really mean and totally regrettable. Like, I'm sure, selfish old Zach would even care whether Beanie went to Mexico or not! Good grief!

"Um, Beanie, have you actually seen Zach lately?" I finally said in a very courteous and controlled manner. She said she hadn't. Then I asked if he even knew about her losing the baby.

"No." Her voice got kind of flat.

"So, do you plan on telling him?"

"Oh, I don't know.... I guess if I see him. And, who knows, maybe he's already heard about it. I think he and Josh might still do stuff together sometimes. Maybe Josh told him."

"Yeah, maybe so. Isn't it ironic that Zach's the one who originally got Josh all excited about the youth group and the Mexico trip, and now Zach's not even around anymore."

"Well, maybe I should let Zach know about the baby." Her voice grew sad, and I knew she was feeling that pain all over again, and I wished I'd never brought this whole thing up.

"Oh, I don't see why, Beanie. Zach never really seemed to care that much about the baby anyway." An understatement, I'm thinking, since Zach wanted the baby killed in an abortion!

"It's not just that, Cate. I'm thinking, maybe if he knows I'm not pregnant anymore, then maybe he'll want to come back to church and stuff. I mean, maybe he's just embarrassed by all this. And you know, he always really liked it there. Remember how much he really liked Clay?"

Now, talk about your self-sacrificing martyrs! This, to me, takes the cake! So I said, "But how's that going to make you feel, Beanie? I mean, do you really want to see Zach sitting there in church or youth group?"

"I don't know...but maybe he needs it, Cate. I mean, who knows, he could really be hurting too."

I thought, yeah, sure, but said nothing.

She continued. "I honestly believe he should know about the baby; it's his right as the father. I'm just afraid that I can't do it."

Then something in my gut tells me what was coming next. Somehow, I just knew that, as Beanie's best friend, it was my responsibility to offer to do this gruesome and loathsome task. I mean, if she was willing to sit in youth group with the selfish jerk, who was I to refuse to go and tell him. "Okay," I finally said. "How about if I go tell him?"

"Oh, would you?"

I laughed without humor. "Of course, you silly ninny, did you really think I wouldn't?" Then I thought of something else. "Hey, Beanie, how about if we make a deal?"

"Sure. What is it?"

"Okay, if I go and talk to Zach, then you must promise

me you'll come on the Mexico trip."

I heard her exhale deeply, a good sign; she was seriously considering my proposal. "Okay, it's a deal, Cate. But you have to report back to me on every single thing that Zach says about the baby and everything. And I want you to be totally honest about it. Deal?"

"Deal."

So now I'm stuck with the unfortunate task of talking to a guy that I'd just as soon run over with my car—except that might get my car all messed up and bloody. And let me tell you, Zach Streeter is NOT worth messing up my car for!

DEAR GOD, PLEASE FORGIVE ME FOR MY HATEFUL HEART TOWARD ZACH STREETER. I'M SURE HE'S YOUR CHILD AND EVERYTHING, BUT I REALLY DO DESPISE WHAT HE DID TO BEANIE. TALKING TO HIM IS ABOUT THE LAST THING ON EARTH I WANT TO DO RIGHT NOW OR EVER. BUT SINCE I MADE A DEAL WITH BEANIE, I GUESS I'LL HAVE TO GO THROUGH WITH IT. BUT MAYBE YOU COULD HELP ME TO BE JUST A LITTLE LESS HOSTILE TOWARD HIM. OR AT LEAST NOT RAISE A FIST OR CARRY A WEAPON OR ANYTHING VIOLENT LIKE THAT. AMEN!

Wednesday, August 1 (you just never know...)

All day at work, I kept wondering how I was going to force myself to go and talk to Zach. I thought about swinging by the park on my lunch break, but then there'd be all these little kids around, and I'm afraid I might say something shocking around them, and it's not their fault. So, I waited until after work, came home, took a cold shower, then called Zach's house, hoping he wouldn't be home. But guess who answers the phone on the very first ring? So, I asked him if he had a minute to talk, and he said someone else needed to use the phone right now. Then, fighting the urge to say fine and just hang up, I asked if he could meet me somewhere to talk. And he agreed to meet at the coffee shop by the high school.

So I drove over, telling myself that I wouldn't chew his head off or say anything hateful or mean, that I would be cool and calm. And the strangest thing is, when I saw him sitting in the coffee shop, a lot of my anger just sort of melted away. I mean, he looked so totally down and out—a beaten man, really. Not at all like the shining track star, on-top-of-the-world Zach that I remembered from just a couple months ago. No, tonight he looked like he was several days past a shave, his hair was stringy and dirty, his clothes looked like he'd slept in them for weeks, and his eyes—oh man, his eyes. I think it was his eyes that really got to me. They had that exact same look that I'd seen in Beanie's—just sort of flat and dead. It was totally weird.

It was like the wind had been taken right out of my sails (sorry about the cliché, but that's just what it felt like), and I didn't even know what to say to him. I bought us each a cup of coffee, and he didn't object, then we

sat down together and I asked how he was doing. He proceeded to tell me his life was just about totally messed
up. Just like that, no pretense, just real honestlike. So I
asked him about his job, and he told me he'd lost it a
couple weeks ago for not showing up on time.

I asked why he didn't show up on time and he just
shrugged; then he looked me right in the eye and said,
"Caitlin, I'm totally messing up my life right now. Just making a complete mess of everything. Now, what do you think
of that?"

I said I thought it was too bad. And you know what? I
wasn't the least bit glad that he was suffering so bad.
Not at all like I'd have thought I'd be. In fact, it was all I
could do not to reach out and give this grunge guy a
great, big hug. So then I asked him if he was doing any
drugs. (I mean, sheesh, all the signs seemed to be there,
missing work, his appearance, his eyes...) And he just nodded, sadly.

Well, my heart just sank and then I let him have it.
"Zach Streeter," I said a little too loudly because a couple
at the next table suddenly looked our way. So I toned it
down. "Why are you doing this to yourself? You have so
much potential, so much to offer. I mean, just a few
months ago you were helping me to straighten out my life
and directing me toward God. Do you remember that?" I
pointed my finger at him and he nodded sadly.

Then I continued, knowing for sure that I sounded
exactly like that preachy "Sister Caitlin" that Beanie
complains about, but somehow I just couldn't help myself.

"So, you've made some mistakes, have you, Zach? Well, now who the heck hasn't? But just because you blow it a couple times doesn't mean you just give up, do you? And what about God, Zach? What about your commitment to Him? You just giving that up too?"

I could see his fingers curling into fists, but not like he was mad exactly, just frustrated maybe. "I know, Caitlin. I <u>know</u> all that stuff. What do you think I've been telling myself every single day?"

"Yeah, but do you ever listen?"

He looked directly at me then and suddenly I could see his eyes were getting moist and I wasn't sure how much I should push this. So I just prayed a quick, silent prayer, asking God to help me out here. I mean, who am I to think I can rescue somebody like this? I suddenly realized I was walking on real shaky ground here. What right do I have to tell anyone else how to live? I mean, what do I know of his struggles, his demons, his fears?

But then I said, "You know, Zach, God has never stopped loving you, not even for a minute. And He will never stop forgiving you either. But you've got to love yourself and you've got to forgive yourself." I think that got his attention somehow, and so I thought I'd better continue. "Now, I'm convinced you're aware of how badly you hurt Beanie, and to be honest, when I came here today, I really wanted to let you have it with both barrels." I shrugged. "But somehow I don't feel that way anymore."

"Probably because you can see how I've done such a great job of beating myself up," he said in a dismal tone.

I nodded. "Maybe. But just the same I wanted to let you know how Beanie's doing. Have you seen Josh lately or heard anything?"

He shook his head sadly. "Actually, I've been out of town a couple of weeks, just hanging with the wrong crowd and messing myself up even more. I came back this morning, hoping I might be able to straighten out before I lose everything." He looked me in the eyes. "And I mean everything, Caitlin."

Then I finally reached over and put my hand on his arm (I couldn't even believe I did it), and then I said (to my own surprise), "Zach, can you please forgive me for judging you?"

He looked shocked. "Geeze, Caitlin, what'd ya mean? You've got every right to judge me. Shoot, I've been a total jerk to your best friend. I've been selfish and irresponsible—"

I held up my hand to stop him. "I know, I know. But I was having some pretty bad thoughts toward you. And now I'm thinking you're sorry about everything that's happened with Beanie."

"Yeah, I'm sorry. You bet I'm sorry. Man, if I could turn back the clock, I would in a minute. I would! I'd do anything to get everything back to where it was last spring, before all that—I mean, even my own life has gone from the highest heights down to the pits of hell. And I know it's my own stupid fault." Then he pounded one fist into the other. "And you know what, Caitlin? Right here and now, I've made up my mind. I'm going to give up that stupid college scholarship. I'm going to get clean, and I'm going to do the right thing and marry Beanie and be a father to my child."

Well, you could've just blown me over and swept me away with a broom! "You're what?"

"Yeah, I've given a lot of thought to what Pastor Tony said—you know all that stuff about how an unborn baby is a real human being and how abortion is murder and—"

Well, I just couldn't let him go on another minute, he was in such pain, and I knew I had no right to drag this whole thing out. So I said, "Wait, Zach. Stop and listen to me. I've got something to say that you need to hear right now." Then I told him the whole, sad story of how Beanie jumped in front of the car to save Oliver and how she lost the baby and everything. And by the end, we were both just sitting there crying. Right there in Starbucks with God and the whole world looking on. I'm sure the couple at the next table thought we'd both recently escaped the loony bin. Then I just looked around to the people who were quietly watching us, although pretending not to and said, "So, did you enjoy the show?" Then I grabbed Zach's hand and tugged him toward the door, calling out as I went, "And wait till you see what we have lined up for next week's episode; same time, same place." And you know what? They all clapped!

Then Zach and I sat in my car and continued to talk for about an hour, just going over lots of little things, asking and answering questions. Then I gave him a ride home since his van got impounded (just another consequence of his recent little rebellious spree). While parked in his drive-way, I told him that I really loved him (as a brother, of course!) and that I would do anything I could to help him out, but that first of all he needed to turn back to God. And he told me that's just what he planned to do. Then he thanked me and said he was glad that Beanie had such a good friend while she was going through all that stuff. And I reminded him I wanted to be his friend too. Then I raced home to call Beanie, but her line was busy, so I started getting this all down into my diary (just in case I start thinking it didn't really happen!).

And anyway, now that I'm back home in my room, do you know what I think? I think God did a real, live miracle tonight! And I'm so amazed that I actually feel like I'm tingling from the inside out. And all I want to do is keep thanking God and praising Him for this unbelievable evening. But first I have to try calling Beanie again!

SIX

Wednesday, August 1 (yes, I know I already wrote today)

Well, I cannot possibly go to sleep until I get the rest of this down.

I got hold of Beanie, finally, and she was totally flabbergasted when I told her everything that happened with Zach (in detail!). She kept asking me if I was making the whole thing up. And to be honest, I almost wondered about it myself, but I know it's true. Anyway, we talked until almost midnight, and I can't even remember the last time I've heard such pure joy in her voice. But what I treasured most about our conversation was the last things she said to me before we hung up.

"Caitlin," she said, "I could tell that you were really down on Zach before, and I don't blame you at all. I mean, sheesh, I should've been down on him myself. But I realize the reason you were so ticked at him was because you care about me."

"That's exactly right!" I said.

"And anyway, I just wanted to reassure you that even if Zach and I do become friends again, I will never, ever make the same mistakes I made last time. Because when I promised God last June to abstain from sex until marriage, I really, truly meant it. And I still do. And even though I am not technically considered a virgin anymore, I've been praying that God would make me a virgin again, at least in my heart, and I've been really trying to believe that He can do that."

"I believe He can do that, Beanie! And honestly, after tonight and after talking with Zach, I really believe God can do all kinds of miracles. I really do!"

"Me too, Cate." And I could just hear the big, old smile in her voice. Then we said good night and promised to get together tomorrow after work. Beanie's not sure exactly what she'll do with regard to Zach just yet, and she doesn't want it to look like she's pursuing him (because she's definitely not), but she wants to extend a hand of friendship, which I assured her he'd probably appreciate. And now I'm going to bed. What a night!

THANK YOU, GOD, FOR DOING A MIRACLE. AND I PRAY THAT YOU WILL CONTINUE WORKING ON ZACH'S HEART. PLEASE SHOW HIM HOW MUCH YOU LOVE HIM AND HOW YOU'VE FORGIVEN HIM AND ALL THE GOOD THINGS YOU HAVE IN STORE FOR HIM. AMEN AND AMEN!!!

Thursday, August 2 (things are looking up)

Today after work, I went by to pick up Beanie and we went out for tacos and to rehash everything that happened yesterday. She was still feeling pretty good, certainly the happiest I've seen her in ages. "I was kind of hoping Zach would call," she said as she picked at her taco. "But I can understand why he wouldn't. But I just hope he's doing okay, Cate. I wish he had someone to talk to."

"What about Josh?" I suggested. "Or Greg?"

"Yeah, maybe we should give them a call and let them know Zach's in need." Then we noticed the pay phone and decided there was no time like the present. I did the calling. Greg wasn't home, but Josh was, and I started telling him what was going on but got interrupted by the pay phone computer voice demanding more money. (Man, those guys are heartless!) Josh asked where I was and offered to come over and talk. So Beanie and I refilled our drinks and waited for him to show up. Then the three of us talked about ways we might be able to help encourage Zach, and I have to admit (only to this diary) that Josh grew in my eyes tonight. Just listening to him really care about someone besides himself and his wanting to help made me see him in a whole new light. But now, I'm telling myself, calm down, Caitlin girl, don't you go getting yourself all worked up—remember your commitment not to date.... But honestly, tonight it was tempting to just put all that behind me when I saw Josh sitting there being so mature and concerned, and okay, good-looking too! But the good news is, I won't succumb! My heart belongs to God and I won't break my promise to Him. And if Josh and I can just be friends, great. And if not, fine. But I'm not turning back. Not at all!

So anyway, Josh decided to head right over and check on Zach tonight (much to our relief), and then he promised to call and tell us how it went. I suggested he call Beanie since I know she's been biting her nails (I mean literally!) over this all day. And then she can let me know what's up. Besides, I just wasn't sure I was up to hearing Josh's voice over the phone tonight, especially when I'm dealing with these recent temptations. I am determined to stick with my vows, no matter how challenging it gets. I know it's for my best. I really do.

DEAR GOD, PLEASE, PLEASE HELP ME TO KEEP MY VOWS TO YOU. I HAVE THE GUT FEELING THAT I CAN'T DO THIS THING ON MY OWN. I'M AFRAID I MAY BE TOO WEAK. BUT I KNOW YOU'RE STRONG, GOD. SO, ONCE AGAIN, I GIVE YOU MY HEART. NOW PLEASE GIVE ME YOUR STRENGTH. AMEN.

Friday, August 3 (stretching time)

So this is how it goes, huh? I ask God to strengthen me in the area of being tempted by Josh and I end up spending the entire evening with him the following night. But let me explain.

First Beanie calls me at work today (which I try to keep short since I'm not supposed to take personal calls) and asks me if I can do something with her and Zach tonight. I say sure, I'd love to, but that I gotta go and hang up.

Then I get home, and there Josh is sitting on my porch drinking iced tea with Ben and my mom. He waves and smiles, and I ask what he's doing there, and he winks at my mom, then quickly explains, "Now, don't come unglued, Caitlin; this isn't a date. Beanie just asked me to pick you up, and we'll go get Zach. Didn't she tell you all about it?"

"Well, she told me about doing something with Zach, but she didn't say much else." And then Josh's face sort of fell, and I realized how rude that sounded. "But that's okay, Josh," I said quickly. "You just took me by surprise. I think it's great that you're coming. Do you mind if I go change?"

"No, take your time. Beanie said we're going to do silly things like putt-par and bumper cars and stuff." Of course, then Ben thought he should come too, and I almost agreed, but then I remembered the serious issues that Zach and I had talked about two nights before and I wanted him to have that kind of freedom tonight if he needed it. "How about another time, Ben?" I said honestly. And to my surprise this seemed to satisfy him.

So we picked up Zach, then Beanie, and although things seemed a little tense at first, it slowly loosened up. And in the bathroom at putt-par, Beanie told me how

Zach had called her today and that they'd had a good, long talk. He'd apologized for everything and explained what had been going on with him the last few weeks. "He seems so changed," she said. "I mean, kind of broken or humbled or something. And not necessarily in a bad way, although I wouldn't wish what he's gone through on anyone." Then I reminded her that she'd been through quite a bit too. "Yeah," she said kind of sadly. "It's too bad that some of us have to learn through our mistakes."

"Well, at least you learn," I said, thinking of how some people (her mom, for instance) never seem to figure it out at all.

We finally ended up at the Dairy Queen, eating these totally gross "designer" banana splits where we picked out all these weird toppings like caramel and blackberries. But we laughed a lot and felt like kids. Then Zach got kind of serious and thanked us all for caring enough about him to reach out to help. "Tonight, thanks to God and people who care, I think I'm going to make it," he said. "But if you'd seen me just a week ago, you probably wouldn't have given me the time of day."

And I have to admit that Zach did look like a different guy tonight, all cleaned and shaven (not the grunger I'd talked to just days ago). And although I'd like to think that his grunged-out appearance wouldn't have put me off, to be honest, if he'd been a perfect stranger looking like that, I probably would've turned around and looked the other way. And that bothers me a lot. And I'm sure that's <u>not</u> what Jesus would do. So I'd like to learn to look at people differently. Not to be so judgmental about outside appearances. Do you think that's possible? Can superficiality ever be completely exterminated? Can a girl who loves cool clothes and thick, glossy fashion magazines ever learn to accept people for who they really are underneath that veneer? I think, with God, I can. And that's my goal. But do you think I can possibly accomplish it before school starts in September?

Saturday, August 4 (friends and friends)

I really would've liked to sleep in this morning but had promised Andrea I'd give her a ride to another car wash fund-raiser. And I'd also invited Beanie, since she now must go to Mexico (remember our deal?). Anyway, I think Andrea was a little grumped out at me because I'd put her off a couple times last week (due to all the stuff with Beanie, which I felt was pretty serious and Andrea should understand). But now I think Andrea thinks she's in competition with Beanie (you know, the old grade school girlfriend triangle stuff), but fortunately Beanie seems to be above that kind of game playing. And I was just trying to be nice to everyone. Even Josh. And by the way, I did <u>not</u> wear my Hawaiian print bikini today (out of respect for Josh's feelings last time). Although Andrea wore hers and naturally managed to pull in a lot of traffic, <u>and</u> (I couldn't help but notice) Josh's glances as well. It figures. But just the same, I'm glad I didn't wear mine.

Just watching Andrea prance around like she was

some Malibu Barbie beach babe made me realize how I probably looked, and it's not an image I wish to perpetuate. (Isn't that a great word? I think it means to keep something going.) Of course, I won't let Andrea know what I think (or at least not in those words), but if she asks I might tell her gently that I think I understand what Josh was talking about. And I still might wear mine for sunbathing in the privacy of my own backyard!

Anyway, as things were winding down, I heard Josh telling Greg about the situation with Zach and saying that it'd sure be cool if Zach could come on the Mexico missions trip too, if there was enough room. And Greg said he'd look into it and that Zach had already earned some money toward the trip last spring. So, who knows, maybe Zach will get to come too.

Sunday, August 5 (one week before Mexico!)

Zach came to church and youth group with Josh today, and it was so good to see him there. Everyone just welcomed him back like nothing had ever happened, and I think Zach appreciated that. I mean, you can only tell your story about how you've blown it so many times.... Anyway, I saw him talking with Greg after youth group, then Greg gave him a big hug. It feels like Zach's back for the long haul. And that's a good feeling. Beanie has told me that she's trying to keep a distance between them, for his sake as well as hers. She says for the time being, she would rather just be a casual friend, not even a close one, and I think that's wise on her part. In fact, that's how I feel about Josh. And I think he understands.

Greg announced that the Mexico missions group would meet every night this week to prepare for what we'll be doing one week from now. I can't wait!

After church, Andrea and Beanie and I went to a matinee. And surprisingly, it was pretty good and clean too. Maybe Hollywood can do films for those of us who aren't into all that gratuitous sex and violence—wouldn't they be surprised to know that we're out here? Then we decided to do something a little weird. (It was Beanie's idea and was actually inspired from a scene in the movie, which was about doing random acts of kindness). And to our surprise, Andrea wanted to come along and do it with us. At first I thought it was because she didn't want to be left out, but when it was all said and done, I think she just wanted to help. Sometimes I think I'm too hard on Andrea, too judgmental and harsh (probably because she's a lot like me and sometimes people just assume girls like us are totally shallow and superficial, which we can be, of course, but not always!).

Anyway, this is what we did. I drove over to Beanie's mom's house. We weren't sure if she'd even be home or not, but thankfully her car was gone. And Beanie (who still has a key to the door) let us in. And, oh man, that place was worse than ever, and for a minute I felt really sorry and embarrassed for Beanie. (I mean, because Andrea was there, and I'm sure Beanie felt totally humiliated by this.) But you know what Andrea said: "Hey, your mom and my dad would make a perfect couple!" Then

she explained what a slob her dad was and how she and
I had played maids at the cabin (the weekend that
Beanie thought I was off having the time of my life!),
and we all had a good laugh!

Then we rolled up our sleeves, and like three white
tornadoes, just attacked the place (taking turns to keep
an eye on the driveway in case Lynn popped in). I had
parked my car down the block (not that Lynn would even
recognize it), and if Beanie's mom were to suddenly come
home, our plan was to take off out the back door, hop
over the fence, and sprint through the neighbor's yard.
Anyway, we spent over three hours there, and I've never
seen that little place look so good. When we finished, we
were so proud that I wished we'd brought a camera
along and taken before and after photos. (We might
have won some contest or at least had good résumés for
housecleaning services; not that I'd like to make a
career of that, especially after today!) Anyway, we were
just putting a note beneath a little vase of flowers that
Beanie had somehow scrounged from the weed-infested
flower beds (our next project perhaps?). We'd had Andrea
write the note (so the handwriting wouldn't be recog-
nized) saying God Loves You! And that's when we heard
her car in the driveway. Well, you should've seen us—bolting out the back door, across the lawn, over the fence,
and making a beeline to my car, and off we went. Lynn
never even saw us. We were laughing so hard, I could
barely drive straight. Now, talk about fun!

After that, Andrea invited us to cool off in her pool.

Now, I didn't even know she had a pool, and she acts like it's no big deal. But let me tell you, Beanie and I both thought it was a big deal, and I think she liked that. So we laid out in the late afternoon sun, taking dips, and praising each other for what we'd accomplished today.

And all that friction of the girlfriend triangle just seemed to disappear. But you know what the best part was? I think Beanie was having the absolute time of her life. I mean it! She just sparkled like a diamond. And I think Andrea was impressed with her. I mean, before today, I think she always thought Beanie was kind of a loser chick. And I admit, Beanie did look quite a bit like a loser. But today I think Andrea could finally see what it is I so love about Beanie. And I think that made Beanie feel pretty good too. And when you've had things as hard as she has, feeling good's not such a bad thing! Not at all!

SEVEN

Monday, August 6 (whazzup?)

Today I'm at work, about to take my lunch break (which is only thirty minutes since I'm just part-time) and suddenly Aunt Steph shows up with this funny look on her face, and I'm thinking, oh no, something must be wrong! But she tells me nothing's wrong; she just wants to talk to me. And so, like a couple of regular working women, we go and have lunch (and Rita, the main receptionist, says I can take extra time since I hardly ever take my breaks anyway).

So, we sit down to lunch at this cool little deli down the street and I ask her what's going on. And then she tells me something I really don't want to hear. "Now, you can't tell anyone this," she begins. "But Beanie has given her Mexico scholarship to Zach—"

"What?" I demand. "She can't do that. That was for her—"

"I know, honey. Tony told me all about it. He was hoping we might come up with a way to work this out. But I

wanted to let you know before you heard it from someone else."

Well, now I'm feeling just like someone reached over
and popped my pretty balloon. (Yes, another overly used
metaphor, but I'm in no mood for creativity at the
moment.) "But I really, really want Beanie to go," I com-
plain, knowing I sound just like a spoiled brat. "I mean, I
worked so hard to get her to go and everything." Whine,
whine, whine.

Steph pats my hand and smiles. "I know you did,
honey, and it was so good of you. But don't you think it's
awfully kind of Beanie to give up her trip for Zach? I
mean, she's told me all about his recent changes and
everything, but considering what he did to her before—
the way he treated her—well, I just think it's really gracious and generous on her part. And I'm really proud of
her."

Yeah, sure, I'm thinking, still not convinced this is such
a good idea, but hating to sound all negative. "It's not
that I don't want Zach to go," I try to explain. "I just
really, really want Beanie to come."

"Well, there may be a way for them to both go." She
pauses as if deciding whether or not to tell me. "Tony
asked me not to say anything just yet, but I can see how
upsetting this is for you. So, if you promise not to tell..."

I hold up my hand like a good girl scout (which I never
was). "I promise."

"Okay. There's a slim chance they might both get to
go. Tony's checking on something right now. He should know

before you guys have your first meeting tonight."

Now I'm slightly relieved. "Oh, I sure hope so. And you know I could probably contribute some more money too. Heck, I really don't need any school clothes—"

Now Steph is laughing. "No, I think you've given enough. Let someone else help out. You know that it really is more blessed to give than to receive. Let's allow someone else this blessing."

I grin at her. "You know, Steph, I think you'd make a great pastor's wife."

I can see her blushing, but she gives me this sort of sly look that tells me I might not be too far off the mark, then says, "You just better keep those thoughts to yourself. You know how rumors can get started at a small church like ours."

Now I laugh. "Get started? You better open your ears, Sister Steph, they've been circulating for some time now!"

So anyway, we finished eating lunch, and she promised to call me as soon as she heard anything, one way or another. "And don't forget to pray," she said as we both went our separate ways.

Now, when I got back to work, I suddenly remembered something. Back when I first applied for this job I told Rita how I needed time off in August for this missions trip, and she had mentioned that the corporation sometimes donated to worthy causes and might even contribute to the Mexico trip. But because of my birthday present from my parents, working at fund-raisers, and my job, I'd never needed to ask. So, I decided, why not ask today?

And so I told Rita the whole story, swearing her to
secrecy about Beanie and Zach. And she smiled and
said she'd see what she could do. Then I sent my dad a
quick e-mail note, telling him about the whole thing too,
hoping he might have a little clout he could use to help
out. And he e-mailed right back saying he'd do whatever
he could and had a meeting with one of the bigwigs in a
few minutes anyway.

Well, by the end of the day, Rita marched triumphantly over to the little desk I use to help her stick
labels on envelopes and things like that, and she said,
"We did it!" And I just jumped up and hugged her so tight
I knocked her glasses right off her nose.

"Oh, thank you, thank you, Rita!" I cried. "You don't
know how much this will mean to everyone."

"Just one thing, the big boss says you have to bring
back lots of photos and make a poster or some kind of
display to put up in the lunchroom so everyone can see
what you kids did while you were down there. Is that a
problem?"

I laughed. "Not at all. I think it's a great idea!"

Then she looked at her watch. "Well, your day's
almost over. Why don't you just take off. I'm sure you'd
like to tell your friends the good news."

"Thanks so much, Rita! You're just like the fairy godmother!"

She pretended to wave her wand. "Well, then off
with you!"

But instead of leaving, I went straight up to my dad's

office. Of course, he'd already heard the good news, but he let me use his phone to call Pastor Tony and Steph. And they both agreed to handle everything (which I liked—it feels better to remain sort of anonymous in these things, and I think that's how God likes us to be anyway). Then I drove over to Steph's apartment where I found Beanie and Oliver watching <u>Sesame Street</u> together.

"Sheesh, Bean, I think you're getting a little old for this," I said as I flopped down on the couch with them and immediately started making fun of Big Bird (whom I used to totally adore as a child), but I was just trying to conceal my pleasure of this latest bit of good news.

"Hey, don't knock it. It's a pretty good show, and I never got to watch it as a kid. Oliver and I've learned all kinds of things from these puppet guys."

I could tell she was trying to cover for feeling down, and suddenly I felt guilty for not telling her the good news right then and there, but at the same time was still a little irked that she'd almost given away (albeit unwittingly) the gift <u>I'd</u> given specially to her. "So, you want to grab some burgers before the missions meeting tonight?" I suggested without looking her in the eye.

"Uh, that's right," she said slowly, focusing her attention on Oliver's curly hair. "Uh, I almost forgot to tell you. I can't go on the trip."

"You <u>can't</u> go?" I jumped up from the couch, acting pretty upset (you know how Beanie loves drama, or used to anyway). "What do you mean you can't go? Why can't you go? I thought it was all settled and everything."

"Well, I just can't go, that's all. I'm sorry. But I know you'll have a great time. And Andrea will be there for you to hang with—"

"Beanie! Andrea is <u>not</u> you! Now, don't you remember you promised me you'd come? We had a deal. <u>Remember</u>?"

Her dark eyes got really big. "Oh, Cate, I forgot all about that. Oh, I'm so sorry."

To my huge relief, Steph walked in right then. And I turned toward her and, with a wink, said, "I can't believe her, Steph! Beanie's telling me she can't go on the Mexico missions trip now, and she promised me—"

Beanie came up from behind. "Oh, I'm so sorry, Caitlin!" I could hear a sob in her voice and I turned around to see great big tears streaming down her cheeks. And let me tell you, I felt like a total crud bucket about then.

"Hang on a minute, everyone," called Steph as she swooped up Oliver who was watching us both with that typical toddler, wide-eyed curiosity. "Beanie," said Steph, "I just spoke to Tony, and it's all worked out. You <u>can</u> go! The problem is solved. And Zach can go too."

Beanie just seemed to melt in relief about then, and feeling like an absolute lowlife slimeball, I threw my arms around her. "Oh, I'm so glad you're coming! I really wanted you to come."

She wiped her nose on her baggy sweatshirt sleeve. "I wanted to come too. I really did."

"Well, you better go change then, unless you want to

go to the missions meeting looking like the baby-sitter queen. And if you hurry, we'll still have time to grab a burger before it starts."

She dashed off and I rolled my eyes at Steph. "I can't believe what an idiot I can be sometimes," I said quietly as I poured myself a glass of water. "I was just trying to be dramatic."

Steph laughed. "Well, maybe Beanie's had enough drama to last her a while."

I nodded. "No doubt."

"And good job on <u>blessing</u> that corporation," she whispered as Beanie came out looking fresh and pretty in a sundress and sandals.

"Gosh," said Beanie as she pecked little Oliver on the cheek. "I feel just like Cinderella, getting to go to the ball after I'd given up all hope."

I laughed but wisely didn't mention that Rita at work had just been playing fairy godmother.

Sunday, August 12 (for Clay!)

After a whirlwind week of working and missions meetings and Spanish tapes and packing and repacking (we can only take one big suitcase and one small bag), we finally loaded all twenty-seven of us onto a big bus this morning (after a quick prayer meeting where half the congregation came to show their support). And now we're off! <u>Ariba</u>! <u>Ariba</u>! (which means "hurry up"). But as a consequence of this incredibly hectic week, I've missed writing in my diary, but now plan to keep careful notes (and take lots of photos) during the entire trip.

And I do want to take a moment to note here how we've dedicated this whole trip to Clay Berringer's memory. We all feel if it hadn't been for him, we wouldn't even be going now. And while Pastor Tony was praying for us this morning, it was almost as if we could feel Clay's presence with us. And all week long, while we've been going to meetings and struggling with our Spanish, or whatever challenges, we've all started this habit of raising a victorious fist and saying "For Clay!" So I guess that's the motto for our trip—For Clay! And of course, we know it's for Jesus (we're not stupid or starting some cult or anything), but it's because of the way that Jesus used Clay's life to touch ours that we think maybe our lives can be used to touch those people in the village where we're heading.

We've been praying for some of these people all week. We even have a list of names to pray for—not everyone, but quite a few. A local pastor wrote them down for us so we could pray for real names like Juanita and Miguel and Hernando and Maria. Our main mission is to help at an orphanage, to build and repair some buildings, and work with the orphan kids and stuff. And just last night, Greg (our fearless leader) gave us this little speech about how we need to be prepared for anything and everything and how this trip wasn't for the faint of heart. As if we were thinking we were heading off to Club Med for some fun in the sun! But we all soberly reassured him that we were up to the task. No slackers here!

And right now everyone on the bus is singing real loud,

so (not wanting to appear unenthusiastic, especially at the onset of this important mission) I'll have to sign off and join the group! _Adios_, _amigos_!

EIGHT

Monday, August 13 (run for the border!)

After many hot and grueling hours of
travel (just barely out of town, our old Greyhound
totally blew its air-conditioning unit!), we have actually
crossed the border into Mexico! Ole! We went through
Tijuana about an hour ago, stopping for a late lunch at a
church that was expecting us and threw quite a grand
little fiesta with all kinds of fantastic Mexican food. And
they had a guitar and brass band, and then we sang a
couple songs for them and they all gathered around us
and prayed for our mission. Really sweet people. It's amazing how you can meet someone you've never seen before;
you don't even speak the same language (well, just
barely); and you'll probably never see them again (at
least this side of eternity); but somehow you just instantly
bond with them, like your hearts just totally understand
each other. Well, only God can do that!

Now the bus is all quiet (and hot) and most of the
kids are snoozing. We slept in sleeping bags on a church
floor last night, and I don't think anyone got a whole lot of

rest. But for some reason I'm wide awake. Too excited, I guess. And, to be honest, a little cranky.

Here's why. Well, we start out this trip and Beanie and Andrea and I are all hanging together. Not that we're ignoring others, but we've kind of like the three amigos (or so I think). But last night after we had a potluck at the church, we got to go play at a water park to cool off (okay, so going on a Mexico mission isn't all hard work and sacrifice), but anyway, Andrea (who _did_ bring her Hawaiian bikini) seemed to be flirting with Josh (who despite his earlier judgments did seem to appreciate that bikini after all—meanwhile ol' Cate's wearing her sensible one-piece!). Anyway, before the night's over, it seems like Andrea and Josh are kind of pairing off. Okay, there was no touching or kissing or anything like that going on, but today on the bus they're sitting together, and right now she's sleeping with her head on his shoulder. Now, why does this make me so grumped out? Maybe I'm just hot and tired. I'll try to get some sleep. And now it seems that Andrea has been replaced by Zach (who's being very sweet, by the way), so I guess maybe it'll be Beanie and Zach and me (the new three amigos).

Tuesday, August 14 (we're here!)

We got in late yesterday afternoon and they had a sort of welcome dinner for us (although we got the privilege of cleaning up afterwards). Then we were assigned rooms and stuff. Beanie, Andrea, me, and Tricia (a quiet girl from McFadden that I've been trying to reach out to) are all sharing a room that's about ten by ten (we have bunk beds) and pretty tight. I'm sleeping up and Beanie is down. (I get too claustrophobic down there, but it's hot up here.) We've already in bed (only 9:30) but the generator goes off at ten, and then other than flashlights it'll be completely dark. But I don't think anyone minds too much, we're pretty tired and we're supposed to be up at six!

We've only seen part of the compound but it seems pretty big. This was a mission that was originally set up as an orphanage (thousands of kids are orphaned in Mexico every year). But it's grown into quite a bit more than that. And tomorrow we'll have the full tour and get our job assignments. Beanie and I both asked to work directly with the young children. Andrea wants to be on the construction crew (but I think it's because that's what Josh is doing). Tricia is working in the kitchen compound. And Zach offered to work with the older kids (he has experience with this). So we'll see how it goes.

Thursday, August 16 (really hard stuff)

I was too exhausted yesterday to write anything. Man, I've never been so tired in my life. I'm not sure if it's all physical either, because I'm starting to feel pretty emotionally strung out too (especially after today).

But let me back up. Yesterday, Beanie and I worked with the preschoolers in the orphanage. It was really fun (but hard work). They're all so sweet and they like lots of attention, which meant we were lifting and holding them a lot. But it was fun. I just fell in love with this one

little girl, Rosa. I wish I could take her home. I really do.
I've considered calling my parents and asking. But the
orphanage supervisor (an older woman from Texas named
Clara) said most of the kids there were "unadoptable." I
didn't ask why yet, but I will. Anyway, little three-year-
old Rosa is a sweetie pie. And she's so shy. I think that's
what caught my attention. She always hangs around
the fringe of the group, and it took all day, but finally I
got her to get involved in a craft project. Then she sort
of attached herself to me. And it was so sweet. And this
morning, she came right to me and lifted up her chubby
brown arms for me to pick her up. I almost cried with joy I
was so happy.

So anyway, the plan today was to spend the morning
in the orphanage and then to go over to another one
closer to the town. This orphanage wasn't so nice (crummy
building with leaky metal roof, outhouses for bathrooms,
and only one sink with running water). But apparently
they're doing the best with what they can afford right
now and have plans for a better facility. Anyway, Beanie
and I decided to spend some time doing some cleaning (it
sure needed it and no one complained!), and we even
tried to get the kids involved too (which got a little
messy a couple of times), but I think they had fun. And
when we finished, it did look better. Then on our way
back to the main compound (we get to ride in this funky
old Volkswagen Beetle that looks like it's about to fall
apart), our guide, Alex Little (a college-aged kid whose
parents are part of the mission), asked if we wanted to

stop by the dump. Well, we just sort of laughed, like we thought he was kidding. But he was completely serious. We asked why. And he said because that was part of the mission's outreach too, although due to lack of funds was somewhat neglected. So we said sure, why not?

Oh man, now let me tell you, if you ever want to have your heart just ripped right out of your chest and twisted until you think you're going to die, just go to a Mexican garbage dump. And, yes, it smells horrendous, but that's not what I'm talking about. You see, in Mexico (and apparently a lot of impoverished countries) the poorest of the poor people hang out at the garbage dump. Whole families live there! And they build these sad little huts out of debris of cardboard or metal or whatever they've managed to scrounge from the big, stinking pile of refuse. And then whenever fresh garbage comes in (and we're talking Mexican garbage) these scrawny, dirty, little kids scramble all over the putrid, smelling heaps, digging like desperate animals to find a scrap of moldy tortilla or a rotten apple core or whatever piece of trash that might appear edible to them.

Oh man, I just wished I'd had some food on me to toss their way. And fortunately, Alex did. He'd thought to bring along a jar of peanut butter and a loaf of bread (apparently he does this a lot), and man, you should've seen that stuff disappear. Talk about a feeding frenzy. And afterwards Alex led the kids in a couple of songs in Spanish—"Jesus Loves Me" and another one I don't know yet.

But here's what totally shames me, and it hurts to even write this down. I didn't want those kids to touch me. I mean, here I've been with little orphan kids all day. And sure, they were kind of dirty and smelly, but relatively clean—compared to these. These poor little dump kids were incredibly filthy (like they'd never been bathed their whole lives) and smelling like something I can't even begin to describe and would like to forget, and (I'm sorry, God!) just totally disgusting. And their little heads are shaved and bald. Alex said it keeps the lice down, but you can hardly distinguish the girls from the boys. And their tattered clothing is so filthy from crawling around in the trash.

But I'm so ashamed that I really did not want to touch them, or for them to touch me. And it makes me feel like a selfish creep. Fortunately, Beanie handled it much better than I did. She's so amazing. She got right down on their level and talked to them, and even touched them. But I just stood there like a pillar of ice. I just did not want to touch them. (Oh, forgive me, God!) And even as I'm writing this I can't stop crying. Everyone here thinks I'm totally losing it today. And maybe I am. I didn't go to dinner. I mean, how can I possibly eat when there are little kids literally starving out there tonight? I don't know if I'll ever be able to eat again!

And while I'm confessing about what a complete wimp and a creep I am, as soon as we got back, I had to go take a shower. I felt so unclean from just seeing those children. And then I just never wanted to come out of the shower. And as hard as I scrubbed, I felt like I'd never be clean again—ever! Oh, I just don't know what's wrong with me. And I don't know if I'll be able to take this for nine more days. Oh, why did I ever come to this horrible place?

OH, GOD, PLEASE, PLEASE HELP ME! I AM UNABLE TO DO THIS. I FEEL MY HEART IS BROKEN. OH, WHY DO YOU ALLOW SUCH SADNESS IN THIS WORLD? AND WHY DID I HAVE TO FIND OUT ABOUT IT NOW? PLEASE HELP ME OR I WON'T BE ABLE TO DO THIS.

Friday, August 17 (I survived another day)

At breakfast today (yes, I was actually able to eat again), I just looked around at all these kids (my friends), and I couldn't understand how they could laugh and smile like there weren't these little kids starving just miles away. And I tried to act like I wasn't hurting inside, but let me tell you, I was. And I am. I don't think I'll ever get over this. I feel like I'm constantly on the verge of tears.

But I suppose it helped to be working back in the compound preschool today. These kids are clean because they get bathed daily. In fact, today, Beanie and I got to help with that. And I didn't mind touching these kids at all. It was even kind of fun to wash their dark curly hair. And I didn't even mind doing a lice check (okay, it bugged me a little at first), but we didn't find a single nit. (That's what the eggs are called that get attached to their hair.) Anyway, these kids wear fairly nice clothes that are donated from American churches and laundered here on the compound regularly. (You should see their laundry facility, really state of the art, thanks to a generous church in Columbus, Ohio.) These kids seem really happy and healthy despite the sad lot life seems to have dealt them. In fact, as we went around the compound today, I couldn't help but notice how everyone here seems to be really and truly happy. Everyone but me, that is.

My philosophical friend (Beanie) says it's all relative. That the people being helped by the mission may seem poor by our standards, but they remember how life used to be much worse for them and they appreciate every little thing they've got now. I suppose she should know since, in some ways, she's had a pretty hard life too. I think she probably felt like an orphan quite a bit while she was growing up (even though she had a mom and a home). Then I asked her what she thought about the garbage dump kids. She got kind of quiet, then said she felt bad for them. I knew I wouldn't be able to say how I felt without breaking into tears, so I just kept it to myself, but I know she understands because she reached over and gave me a hug.

And even though I'm doing better today, I just couldn't bring myself to go to the sing-along tonight. After dinner, I asked Beanie and Zach to tell Greg that I wasn't feeling well (which isn't untrue) and then I slipped back to our room, which is hotter than Hades tonight. But I don't really care. Tonight I'm going to do nothing but pray for those garbage dump kids. It's the only thing I know how to do at the moment. And so that's what I'm going to do. I'm not trying to be a saint (ha, the saints would be ashamed of me for the way I wouldn't let those kids touch me!), but I feel like this is what I need to do tonight.

DEAR GOD, I DON'T EVEN KNOW QUITE HOW TO PRAY. BUT I WANT TO COME TO YOU ON BEHALF OF THOSE KIDS AT THE DUMP. FOR SOME REASON I CAN'T STOP THINKING ABOUT THEM. AND SO I THINK I'D BETTER PRAY FOR THEM. PLEASE, SHOW ME HOW TO PRAY....

NINE

Sunday, August 19 (day of rest?)

They try to keep Sundays as a "day of rest" around here, but the problem is there is still lots of work to be done when there are so many children with so many needs. So we all pitched in this morning, then we went to church service (where our youth group sang several songs for the congregation), and now we pretty much get to spend the remainder of the day as we please. Right now, we're in our room having a little quiet time before we all hop in the bus and drive over to the beach (which is about an hour from here).

Thankfully, I'm feeling a little more peaceful about the situation here. I have learned (through Alex) that many of the "orphans" here at the compound are originally from the garbage dump. And that's why so many are unadoptable—they still have living parents. And although their parents (according to Alex) may be serious drug addicts or mentally ill or just basically unable to care for a child, they will not sign away their parental rights to their children. And the parents don't seem to

care that this deprives their child from ever being
adopted into a loving family or into a better life. Alex
says it's because Mexicans basically have a very strong
sense of family and heritage, and even if they can't
care for their own, they don't really want to give them up
either. If you ask me, it's pretty selfish on the part of
these parents, but then I probably don't really understand their culture very well yet. Anyway, this explanation did help me to feel better about the dump kids, like
maybe they'll have a better situation before long. Alex
says that many of them will wind up here eventually. The
problem is the mission doesn't have enough room and
finances to support all the local children. That's why
they've developed that shabby "annex" orphanage we
visited. And their plan is to create more and more orphan-
ages, but they can only do so much for the time being. Or
as so many of the people say—mañana (that means
later). Everything around here is mañana—meaning we'll
get to that later. I just wish later could come sooner.

So this is my plan. When I go home, I'm going to get
everyone I can to send money down here. And I plan on
doing my part too. And maybe, just maybe, we can make
a difference for some of those kids out at the dump.

But for the rest of this afternoon, I will try not to
dwell on these things. My friends are thinking I'm all
depressed and moody. So I'll try to put on a happy face.
Especially where Josh and Andrea are concerned,
because Andrea is acting all sorry toward me, like I'm
jealous that she and Josh are an "item." Which is totally

ridiculous. Okay, maybe I was a little concerned at first, and yes, it tweaks me just a little even now, but somehow in light of the desperate needs of these poor, starving children, Josh and Andrea's love life (or whatever it is) just seems a trifle insignificant to me. And so I plan to laugh and smile a lot for the rest of the day.

Tuesday, August 21 (a big step for me)

Today Beanie and I went to the annex orphanage to help out again (our third time there). And it's amazing because <u>today</u> it seemed a whole lot better to me. I mean, it's still a shaky old rickety building with outhouses and everything, but <u>today</u> I could see how it was really a great place for all those kids to be (maybe because I was comparing it to the dump). But I mean, these kids get real food (okay, mainly beans and rice and a little fruit and milk), but they also get health care (a real nurse comes out once a week). And they have these little cots to sleep on with sheets that are fairly clean. So compared to the dump, it's like staying at the Ritz. They even have toys to play with. (Sure they're not the greatest, but better than old tires and rusty tin cans.)

So anyway, before we drove the Bug over there, I stopped by the kitchen to beg a jar of peanut butter and a loaf of bread, and while the main cook wasn't looking, Beanie even threw in a few oranges that were getting slightly spongy as well as some dark-skinned bananas. And after we finished at the orphanage, guess where we went?

Beanie looked at me kind of skeptically and asked, "You sure you're up for this, Cate?"

"Yeah," I answered as I determinedly drove the Bug over the lumpy, dusty road. The dust around here is so thick it coats you like a scaly skin, even your teeth get all gritty from it. "I _need_ to do this, Beanie."

"Okay." She still didn't sound convinced. "I just don't want you to fall apart on me. I don't even know how to drive a stick shift. If you go to pieces, we might just have to spend the night here."

Ugh, the thought of being stuck at the dump all night literally made my skin crawl! But I tried not to show how badly her words affected me. "I'll be fine, Beanie. This is something I need to do. Like conquering your fears, you know?"

"Yeah, but maybe we should've brought Alex too."

I considered this. She might be right. "Well, why don't we just say a prayer on our way. I think God can help us do this." So Beanie prayed as I drove, and suddenly I wondered if this wasn't such a good idea after all.

So there we are, barely out of the car, and the kids begin flocking over to us. As fast as I can, I begin smearing peanut butter on bread slices while Beanie attempts some crowd control. And I must admit I probably wasn't as fast as Alex (he's had lots more experience). But one by one, I manage to hand the pieces out to the grubby little hands, not even cringing as their skinny, filth-encrusted fingers touch mine. They remind me of brown birds, scrappy and grabby and worried they might not get their fair share. But somehow (not unlike the story of loaves and fishes) all are fed. How quickly the bread and peanut butter disappear! Then I remember the fruit in the car. But I think perhaps first we should sing a song or two (like Alex had done).

And so we all sit in a circle (right there in the gross dirt that fringes the dump), and the children cooperate beautifully. (I'm sure to show their appreciation for the food and in the hope that there might be more.) So we sing several songs (in Español, no less), ones that Beanie and I learned at the preschool, and then we teach them a couple of finger-plays that we did with the preschoolers each day. This seems to delight the children, and one little girl (I'm pretty sure she is a girl because she seems to have on what may have once been a dress) actually climbs into my lap. And—here's the miracle—I don't really mind. (Okay, maybe a little at first, but then I am all right, really!) Then I mentally count the heads in our circle of children and realize there will not be enough fruit for everyone to have their own piece, so I know we need to divide it up.

I explain my concern to Beanie, and we both reach into the bag and each take out an orange and begin peeling. The children watch us with wide, hungry eyes as we separate the orange sections, juice dripping on our hands. Then one by one, we hand the pieces out to the kids. We do this over and over until all the fruit is gone. Then I show the children the empty bag and hold up my hands saying, "No hay más."

So then we're not really sure what to do next. We stand up with the kids all clamoring around us, like they don't want us to leave or are hoping we'll pull another bag of food out of the car. And that's when I notice several suspicious (and I must admit sinister) looking men gathered nearby, standing just outside the circle of children, and probably wondering what two gringo girls are doing out at the garbage dump and alone. And that's when it occurs to me that they may think nothing of mugging and robbing us and throwing us onto the garbage heap as they make off with our little car. I mean, after all, these people have absolutely nothing, and like Alex said, some are serious drug addicts who'll do just about anything for their next hit. So now my heart's starting to race as one of the men begins to move closer, a dark look in his eye. And then, all of a sudden, I just start singing "Jesus Loves Me" again, and I reach out to take the hands of the two kids nearest to me. And Beanie, who I can see has also become aware of this potential danger, follows my lead, and pretty soon we're all holding hands in this little circle and singing for all we're worth. And it's really pretty cool. The kids are having a good time.

And that's when I look, and I <u>really see</u> these little upturned and dirty faces of these same children who had so appalled and disgusted me only one week ago. And today, I swear, they look just like angels. Well, maybe I'm just so overwhelmed with fear that I'm actually hallucinating, I don't know for sure. But when I look at what I'd seen before as dump kids with their shaved heads and dirt-encrusted faces, all I can see now are these beautiful dark-eyed angel children. And I'm just totally humbled and astonished. And I think to myself, is it possible that God is allowing me to see them the way He does? Could that even be? I mean, it's almost like supernatural or something totally unearthly. I still get goose bumps just thinking about it.

But, okay, here's another really weird thing about this little event: I don't even remember how Beanie and I moved away from the circle of children, climbed back into the car, and then drove safely away from the dump. I mean, I can't actually remember finding the keys, starting the engine, or anything. And she doesn't either! Pretty weird, huh? But somehow we did. And if you ask me, I'd say it was a total miracle! In fact, the whole thing at the dump from beginning to end just seemed like one great, big wonderful miracle. I totally give God the credit and thank Him for it!

Not only that, but Beanie and I plan to go back to the dump as many times as possible during the next three days. And (I haven't told Beanie or anyone else) I plan to use my own spending money to buy some food and things for those kids. But we decided the next time we go, we'll invite Alex and anyone else who wants to come along too. Miracles like this must be meant to share!

Thursday, August 23 (one more day at the mission)

I can't believe we have only one more full day at the mission (tomorrow). I remember how when I first got here, I was so freaked that I'd wimp out and they'd have to ship me home, and now I don't even want to leave at all. We've been to the dump two more times since that last visit (both times Zach came too!). And while nothing so incredibly miraculous has happened, it was still fun seeing the kids. They know us by name now, and I can tell they really appreciate our visits. Alex and I went into town today, and I used my own money to get food (two whole boxes of staples including lots of peanut butter), and Alex has promised to take just a little out at a time. He's worried if we take the whole thing out there, some of the adults will confiscate it from the kids and go trade it for drugs. So I agreed to let him handle it. I also promised to raise more money at home to send for this specific purpose. And Alex promised to find someone who could continue this when he goes back to college in the fall. (I learned through someone else that he's a Stanford premed student, but he spends his vacation times down here—pretty impressive if you ask me.)

We'll have one last visit to the dump tomorrow, and Zach says he won't miss it for anything. On the first day he went out, I was so impressed with how he just reached out and shook their dirty little hands without even pausing. I still feel guilty to think how badly I reacted at first. But then, I'm only human, and God sure helped me get over my fears.

Beanie and I have been checking each other for lice every night (after we take our showers and thoroughly wash our hair). Tricia and Andrea tease us without mercy, saying we look like a couple of apes picking parasites from each other, but we've yet to find an actual sign of lice or anything. And I'm a little miffed with Andrea for not wanting to come out to the dump with us. Tricia can't help it since she's desperately needed in the kitchen at that time of the afternoon. But I thought, at least Andrea and Josh could make a better effort. I mean, all they've done is work on construction sites, and even though I know they're working hard, and Andrea keeps complaining about all her blisters and aches and pains, it just doesn't seem to me they've had all that much contact with the people. But I suppose that's kind of judgmental on my part. So I won't bug them anymore.

Saturday, August 25 (adios, amigos!)

I can't believe we're done with our mission. Where did the time go? And how will we ever know if what we contributed really made a difference or not? And who will feed the dump kids after Alex leaves next month? And who will hold my little Rosa and count her fingers and toes for her every morning and make her laugh? Oh, I'm so incredibly sad. I'm just keeping my nose in this diary and pretending to be all absorbed in my writing, and yet I can barely see the words because my eyes are so blurred with tears and the pages are getting too soggy to even write upon.

OH, DEAR GOD, PLEASE HELP YOUR CHILDREN. PLEASE HOLD THEM IN YOUR HANDS. PLEASE FEED THEM AND SHOW THEM HOW MUCH YOU LOVE THEM. AMEN.

(later the same day)

I am feeling a little less blue now. Beanie and Zach have been good medicine for me. They understand. Perhaps even better than I do. Because I know both of them have come from difficult home lives. I guess growing up in a fairly secure and happy home, I just didn't fully realize how much pain and suffering there is in this world. But like Zach keeps pointing out, those kids weren't unhappy (at least the ones in the orphanage). And the dump kids weren't really all that unhappy either, they were just hungry and so glad to get food, and they probably will have brighter days ahead. In fact, I'm sure they will because I will not rest unless they do!

And here's something that surprised me yesterday—who do you think joined us to go to the dump? Josh Miller! Yes, at the last minute he came running over and climbed into the backseat next to me and said, "Let's go." But I'm sure he had no idea what he was letting himself in for, and once we were there and he saw what

we'd already become accustomed to, I noticed the
same look on his face that I'd worn a week ago. I tried
not to laugh at him or appear smug because I will never
forget that feeling as long as I live. But a little part of
me was glad or relieved or whatever that someone else
was feeling it too. And even though he tried to be helpful, he mostly just stood around with his eyes wide and
his mouth hanging open. And I'm sure back at the compound he took a really long shower too. But I'll spare his
dignity that much and not ask him about it. Still, I'm glad
he made the effort to come. It's something we all need
to see, even if only once.

So now, back to reality. After hours of driving, we've
crossed the border back into the good, ol' U. S. of A. (And
let me tell you, I'm glad to be coming home again—this is
one great country we live in, and I know I didn't fully
appreciate it before seeing how others live.)

But now, of all things, we're stopping at Disneyland for
the rest of the day and evening. Of course, we all knew
this was our big reward after the mission was accomplished, but somehow it just doesn't seem quite as exciting as it did a few weeks ago. I mean, talk about your
harsh contrasts—starving garbage dump kids, then
Mickey and Minnie dancing down the immaculate streets
of Disneyland! Of course, my dismay might also have
something to do with the fact that I've only got a couple
of bucks left to spend. Oh well, at least my ticket to get
in is already purchased. Greg took care of that before
we ever left home. And have I mentioned that I do miss

home? <u>A lot</u>! I miss Mom and Dad and even Ben (in fact, I miss Ben quite a bit!). Will wonders never cease!

TEN

Sunday, August 26 (on the road again)

Well, I must admit the fireworks show was totally incredible. But to tell you the truth, I felt a little overwhelmed when we first walked into Disneyland today. I mean, everything is so perfect and clean—so vastly different from Mexico. It was like we were on this totally different planet. But it was a great relief to me that I wasn't the only one aware of this difference. In fact, we were getting a bite to eat at (of all things) a Mexican restaurant (Zach and Beanie generously bought me some food after teasing me for having spent all my cash—I didn't tell them <u>what</u> I'd spent it on) when I noticed an overflowing trash can with plates still half full of untouched food. "Wouldn't the dump kids just love that?" I said, and we all started laughing. Except for Andrea, that is. She just looked at me with disgust and said, "Don't be so gross, Cate; some of us are trying to eat here." I glanced at Beanie and we both rolled our eyes. Okay, there I go again passing judgment. (God, forgive me.) But <u>sometimes</u>...

Anyway, I couldn't help but notice Josh's expression

when this all transpired. He didn't say a word, but I could tell he was thinking real hard about something. I'm pretty sure that his visit to the dump yesterday did something in him. And another thing I noticed is that he and Andrea don't seem to be such an item anymore. They haven't even sat together in the bus or anything. And today we're all just hanging together as one group—no coupling off. In fact, maybe that's why Andrea is being such a grump today. I feel kind of bad because it seems like she might've missed out on something important. And I don't mean Josh! I mean something that the rest of us may have discovered in Mexico, something we found at the dump. But I could be all wrong about this too. Who knows?

Well, I better turn off the light and go to sleep. We're staying in a Motel Six tonight, but at least they have a pool and we all got to cool off before bed. It's after one in the morning, we're supposed to be out of here by seven, and my stomach's rumbling. I wonder if I'll have to beg for food tomorrow. But you know what? I don't really care. I think I should go hungry more often, if only to remind myself of how those kids at the dump feel. So even if I don't get to eat a single thing tomorrow, it'll be okay. At least I get to go home where there's food in the cupboards and fridge. Gee, how lucky can a girl be?

THANKS, GOD, FOR TAKING CARE OF ME. PLEASE WATCH OVER THE KIDS AT THE DUMP. AMEN.

Monday, August 27 (close to home)

I can't wait to get home and take a shower and sleep in my own bed. Suddenly I'm realizing how many good things I take for granted every day. Hopefully, I'll be more appreciative of all the "luxuries" we enjoy each day.

This morning, Josh asked if he could sit with me on the bus. And I could tell by his troubled expression that he was just looking for a friend to talk to, so I said sure, and then asked him if something was bugging him. He kind of shrugged like he didn't really know what to say, so I gave it a shot. "Let me guess," I said. "Are you feeling bad after your visit to the garbage dump the other day?"

He turned and looked at me like I was some sort of genius or clairvoyant or something and said, "Yeah, I just can't get the images of those little kids out of my mind."

"I know." I sighed deeply, trying to decide how much of my own feelings I wanted to reveal here, but finally continued. "The first time I went out there it really upset me too. In fact, to be honest, the filth and smell and the way the kids looked actually disgusted me. But at the same time I felt totally rotten for reacting like that—"

"Yeah, that's exactly how I feel."

"So I prayed about it and went out again, and God helped me to see those kids in a whole new light." Well, Josh seemed pretty intrigued, and we had nothing but time to kill, so I decided to tell him the whole story about Beanie and me and the bag of fruit and the malicious looking men. I tried to make it sound sort of humorous, but Josh could see I was serious and I could tell he was really interested.

"That's really cool, Catie." And then he smiled his brilliant Matt Damon smile, and I didn't even start a meltdown. "Thanks for sharing that. You know, I feel so bad for those kids—I mean, I didn't even realize they were there until that last day—and now I just wish I could do something—to help, you know?"

"I know. I feel the same way. Hey, did you get to meet Alex?"

He nodded. "Yeah, he stopped by the construction site a couple times. Seems like a nice guy."

So then I told him about how Alex was going to find someone to regularly oversee some sort of food program for the kids out there and how I planned to find some ways to send money to help out.

"I haven't really told anyone about this yet," I explained. "In fact, I'm not even sure what I'll do. I just know I've got to do something. Maybe through church or more car washes or whatever. I just feel like I need to do this."

"I'd like to help too," said Josh. "I'm not exactly sure how either, especially when I'm heading off to college next week. But I'll see what I can do. And maybe, if you don't mind, I could just send whatever I can pull together your way, and maybe you could sort of manage it for me, if that's okay."

"Sure," I offered. "Anything to help the kids."

"I wish I'd known about that whole thing sooner," he continued. "I would've tried to help out while we were there."

"Well, I tried to tell you guys, but you and Andrea seemed to be in a little world of your own." I know that was uncalled for, and it wasn't exactly jealousy talking (okay, maybe it was a little), but his next words just totally knocked me over.

"Yeah, that whole thing with Andrea was pretty moronic too. And I know I've hurt her feelings by getting involved with her during this trip and then just chilling out on her at the end. I feel really lousy about it."

Well, try as I might, I couldn't think of a single thing to say.

"I can just imagine what you're thinking, Catie, like how dating is so stupid and we should all do what you're doing and no one would get hurt. But what if some of us aren't that strong?"

That made me laugh. "You think I'm strong? Now that's a good one."

"Well, how else do you manage to abstain from all this? I'm pretty positive you're not gay." His eyes twinkled with mischief.

I socked him in the arm but gently. "It has nothing to do with being strong, Josh. It's a promise I made to God, but He's helping me to keep it. And when I see how messed up things get for couples like, say, Beanie and Zach—"

He glanced at where the two were sitting ahead of us, playing some card game on the seat between them.

"They seem to be doing okay now."

"Yeah, now. But they were pretty messed up just a month ago. And I know that Beanie has no intention of ever going back there again."

"So, has she given up dating too?"

I thought about that. "I don't really feel like it's my place to say. You should ask her. But I know she's learned a lot and made some pretty big commitments to God."

I glanced over to Andrea who had her head down, and I knew she was hurting. In fact, I could remember exactly how she felt, and I suppose this emboldened me to say the next words. "You know, Josh, you're a really attractive guy—"

"Gee, thanks." He grinned.

I punched him in the arm again and then continued. "Let me make my point, okay? You know that girls are attracted to you, right?" He nodded. "And I'm sure you enjoy that."

"Yeah. Is anything wrong with that? I've seen guys giving you a second look and you don't seem to mind."

"Yeah, yeah, let me finish. But the difference is you look back. And then you get involved—well, you say you get involved, but the truth is, you're really not involved—or at least your heart isn't—"

"Hey, that's not fair. How do you know what's going on in my heart?"

"Well, take Andrea for instance. You admitted yourself that you got involved with her these last two weeks, but you break up and you're doing just fine, thank you very much. But look at her. Do you think she's doing fine?"

I paused while he looked her way. "No, I guess not. In fact, she told me as much this morning."

"And how does that make you feel?"

"Pretty crummy."

I sighed. "Well, that's a relief. At least you have some feelings—"

"Low blow, Catie. You act like I'm heartless. Do you really believe that?"

I considered this a moment. "Do you want me to be totally honest?"

"Do you think I can't take it?"

I rolled my eyes. "Yes, I'm sure you can take it. I'm just not sure you want to."

"Go ahead, give me your best shot."

"This isn't a contest, Josh. We're just having an honest talk here, right?"

"Yeah, I'm sorry. Go ahead, I'm listening."

"Okay, I think we were talking about how it doesn't bother you to go with a girl then break up—"

"Wait a minute, you're putting words in my mouth. I never said that."

"Maybe not, but like they say, actions speak louder than words. For instance, when I broke it off with you just before the prom, you were back with Jenny the very next day—maybe even sooner."

He didn't answer.

"So, see what I mean? You're one of those guys who can just love 'em and leave 'em. No big deal, right?"

"You're smart about a lot of things, Catie, but you haven't got me completely figured out—not yet anyway."

I smiled. "Good thing too. But my point is, Josh, you have the potential to leave a path of broken hearts strewn along your path. And to tell you the truth, I don't think you're really like that, not deep down anyway. I don't think you _really_ like hurting people."

He nodded. "And you don't think I've ever been hurt before?"

Now I'm sorry, but this made me laugh. "Oh, I'm sure you've suffered some disappointments like in track and stuff like that, but I seriously doubt that you've ever been hurt by a relationship with a girl."

He looked at me curiously, then forced a little laugh himself. "You don't think _you_ hurt me then?"

I stared at him, shocked. Was he serious? "_I_ hurt you?"

"It's not something a guy likes to show or even admit."

For a moment I thought he was pulling my leg, but I could tell by his expression that he was dead serious. "Josh, if I hurt you, I am truly, from the bottom of my heart, sorry. I am. Can you believe that?"

"Yeah." He made a half smile. "So, see? You didn't know me as well as you thought."

I nodded soberly, too dumbfounded to try to figure this conversation all out just yet. "But I guess that just helps me make my point, Josh. You see, I don't want to get hurt in some dating relationship, and by the same token, I don't want to hurt anyone else either. That's why I'd rather just be friends with guys for now. It's so much simpler and no one gets hurt."

"Well, I suppose it's starting to make more sense to me too. But that doesn't mean I'm going to give up girls yet." He grinned mischievously.

"Duh. I didn't expect you to. Besides, I think it's between you and God. I was only trying to make you understand how I think and also how others can get hurt."

"And now you're completely convinced that I _do_ understand, from personal experience that was actually dished out from someone who's since removed herself from the game?"

"Yeah, and like I said, I'm really sorry. I had no idea. I mean, you just seem to snap your fingers and another girlfriend pops up like magic."

"A guy doesn't always want _another_ girlfriend."

"Exactly. Just like I don't want _another_ boyfriend. That's why I'd rather just have a boy for a good friend. To me that's a lot more valuable in the long run."

He nodded. "You might be right." Then he reached out to shake my hand. "Friends? You and me, for the long run?"

I smiled and shook his hand. "You bet. Friends, for the long run."

Then he looked right into my eyes (okay, I knew he wasn't flirting by then, but I did feel my heart give this sharp little tug which I must admit bugged me considerably!) and he said, "Catie, you're quite a gal!"

Well, I just sort of laughed and glanced the other way (not wanting him to have any clue, after all we'd said, that I'd actually felt something beyond friendship) and who should I see staring right at us? <u>Andrea</u>. And let me tell you, if looks could kill, I think I'd be hamburger all over the floor. I tried to smile at her, but I'm afraid it came out more like a smirk (which I didn't intend at all), and now I'll have to go straighten everything out with her later. See, this is just one of those things I hate about this whole guy-girl relationship thing.

Since there seemed to be little else to say, I pulled out my diary and turned toward the window and started writing. Then Josh started talking to Zach, asking about whether he was all ready to head off for college or not. And then it hits me—these guys are moving on—next week even! We won't be seeing them around anymore. And, despite all that's gone on (all the hurts and heartaches), that still makes me pretty sad. To tell the truth, I really do like Josh and Zach a lot. And I'll miss them too.

I wonder if Beanie has considered this. She's sleeping right now. I'm so glad she got to come to Mexico. (And I don't have a single regret for spending a good part of my summer earnings on it.) Having her along reminded me of a side of her that I'd almost forgotten during the last several months—that deep kind of caring compassion that she's always had for people, the way she reaches out to the underdog no matter who they are. And I'd like to think I'm becoming more like that too. If I am, it's only because of God. And for that I say: THANKS, GOD!

ELEVEN

Friday, August 31 (back into the swing of things)

I think I slept for two whole days after we got back from Mexico late Monday night. Mom mercifully unpacked my bags for me and did all my laundry (something she hasn't done in years), but I think she was worried I'd brought home cooties or lice or something infectious (which I suppose is entirely possible). Then on Thursday, I went back to work. (Rita had asked before my Mexico trip if I could cover for her on Thursday and Friday before Labor Day.) But let me tell you, I'm totally beat tonight and really looking forward to three days of doing pretty much nothing (well, maybe a little last minute back-to-school shopping).

On Wednesday night, our church had a potluck dinner for the Mexico missions group. Dad had taken my film in to be developed, and I'd quickly mounted the photos on several pieces of colorful poster board with captions describing what was going on. The potluck was fun, and all the kids shared personal stories about what they'd done at the mission and how it had impacted their lives.

And when my turn came I, naturally, told everyone about the garbage dump kids and all their suffering (probably a little too graphically, but we'd already eaten), and then I shared about my plan to help gather money to send to the mission specifically for those kids. Well, afterwards, it seemed like half the congregation or more came up to me with money in hand, and finally Stephie went and got a coffee can for everyone to put their donations in. Even Josh had managed to get his parents to write a check for $100 and promised to do more later.

Josh and I talked for a few minutes just as the evening was drawing to an end, and he told me about how he'd taken time to call and apologize to Andrea. A relief to me, since I'd already assured her that Josh and I were nothing more than friends and that when she'd seen me with him on the bus, we'd actually been talking about the pitfalls of dating and people getting hurt. At the time, I wasn't too sure she believed me, but maybe now she will.

Then Josh told me he was leaving for college the following day, and he slipped a little handwritten card into my hand with his college address on it. "Do you think you could write to me, Catie?" he asked in a shy sort of way, quickly adding, "Just as friends, of course. I know how you like to write and everything, and I think it'd be fun to hear how you're doing, and what the youth group's up to and all that good hometown stuff."

I assured him, I'd love to correspond. "Just don't get the wrong message if I write some really long letters. I do tend to get carried away with writing sometimes."

"That'd be great. I'll appreciate whatever you send."
Then he said maybe he'd see me at Thanksgiving vacation, and I told him to enjoy college and that I'd be praying for him, and then (to my complete embarrassment) I
got a little weepy, but I think he kind of liked it.

Zach's leaving for college next week too. He seems a
little worried about it. I know he's got a lot on his plate.
Even though he has a full athletic scholarship, he still
has to work to pay for his room and board. I really hope it
goes well for him; he's been through a lot lately. Beanie
told me that they plan to keep in touch with letters too.
"But only as friends," she assured me, as if I've suddenly
become the girl-guy relationship gestapo. Not!

When I got home, I counted out the donations in the
coffee tin—to the grand total of $438.71!!! And I'm think-
ing that'll feed those kids for at least a month or more.

Anyway, I have the phone number of the mission, so I
decided to call with my good news the next morning
before I went to work. Of course, I had to leave a message, asking Alex to return my call, but thankfully, he
hadn't left for college yet and was still down there.

But before he called me back, I put up my Mexico display (poster board and photos) in the lunchroom at work,
along with a tin can for charitable donations that said,
"Feed the Kids" (I'm learning!). And now you wouldn't
believe it, but everyone just kept talking about my photos
and how sad the garbage dump business was, and when I
checked the can at the end of the day on Thursday, it

had $187.34 in it. And by the time I left today it had even more! And I think I'll leave it there for a while to allow everyone at work the chance to be "blessed," as Aunt Steph would say.

So, when Alex called me this morning and I told him I've already collected almost $700 in donations, he's like totally jazzed! He said he has to leave for school soon, but he's got a guy named Hal Royer lined up to take over for him. I met Hal once; he's an older guy who does a lot of maintenance around the mission, kind of quiet, but really sweet spirited, as I recall. So, anyway, Hal is my new contact and everything will be sent care of him. Not only that, but I think I'll put a collection can (with photos) at church every Sunday, and maybe even a box for donating used clothing for kids. And, well, I'm just getting all sorts of ideas. This is going to be fun!

But like I said, I'm really beat right now. And even though it's a Friday night, I'm completely content to stay home and just hang with the family. And I don't think they mind a bit. Dad and Ben went out to rent some videos and pick up a box of Dove ice cream bars (a treat I haven't had since before Mexico), and I'm supposed to make some popcorn, so I'd better get at it!

Sunday, September 2 (is that really you, God?)

I'm feeling a little confused today. Or maybe overwhelmed or perhaps just challenged. I'm just not sure what it is exactly. But I'm feeling something—that's for sure!

Pastor Tony had this friend who's a missionary in Brazil speak in our church today. Kind of interesting, since we've had all this focus on Mexico lately. I guess we're becoming a real internationally aware church. A good thing, I'm sure. Well, at first, I must admit, I was a little wary of this guy because I didn't want him to steal the limelight from the focus on Mexico (more particularly, the garbage dump kids). But as soon as he began to talk, I forgot all about that. For one thing, he mentioned our trip down to Mexico right off the bat and how great it was that we were reaching out to those who were less fortunate (and he even mentioned how important it was that we were giving in order to feed the kids at the dump), and so then I just relaxed and listened.

And man, could this guy keep you at the edge of your seat! Now I'll admit I've never heard a missionary preach before, but I was totally blown away by this guy. (I mean, I'd always thought missionaries were boring, but let me tell you, this one was anything but!) One after the other, he told stories about the drug cartel and amazing miracles and contra rebels and incredible healings, not to mention hundreds of people getting saved all over the place. It seems that just all sorts of things are going on down in South America these days, both good and bad.

So after holding us spellbound for over an hour, he asked us all to bow our heads and close our eyes; then he gave this little invitation—nothing unusual, just offering everyone (who hadn't already) the opportunity to invite Jesus into their hearts. After that he paused for a

few moments, then said he felt a strong impulse to give
another sort of invitation, and that he thought it was for
a young person. He explained how he rarely did anything
like this, but he felt he should today. So anyway, once
again he asked us to bow our heads (for privacy); then
he asked if anyone out there felt God calling him or her
to be a missionary. Well, I can't honestly say I heard God's
voice calling me or anything specific or even audible, but
my heart started to pound furiously, and I felt this <u>really</u>
strong, overwhelming urge inside of me to raise my hand.
And so I did. It was as if I couldn't help but do it.

Well, everybody still had their eyes closed (big relief)
but the missionary guy looked me right in the eye and
said, "I see your hand, my child. And so does God. Don't
worry; He will lead you." And that was it. I lowered my
hand and looked down, and I could still feel my heart
pounding and my cheeks burning as if I'd just admitted
to being the village thief or something. But then the service ended and no one seemed to know what I'd done.
Part of me started saying, "Okay, Cate, just forget about
that whole thing. It was probably just an emotional
response after your missions trip to Mexico." But another
part of me, a stronger part, kept saying, "<u>Oh, my goodness,
this is really for real!</u>"

Now, it's not like I think some big missionary board is
going to come looking for me or that I've been drafted
into the Salvation Army or anything like that. But what
worries me is this: I'm thinking what IF God really is behind
this whole missions thing? What if God is really, truly call-

ing me to be a missionary? I mean, it's just so totally weird. Who would ever believe that Caitlin O'Conner is going to become a missionary? Doesn't it sound totally ridiculous? And for that reason, I'm keeping my mouth shut, at least for now. Besides, I figure, if God is behind this, then (like the missionary guy said) not to worry because He can lead me. Right?

Besides, school starts in two days, and I really need to focus on that right now. So (if it's all the same to you, God) can I just not think about this anymore tonight? Gulp! A missionary?

Monday, September 3 (Labor Day)

Dad said he doesn't understand why Mom and I insisted on shopping on Labor Day (that it's supposed to be a day of rest and all), but we assured him we find fighting the crowds, searching for parking spaces in a hot parking lot, and then sniffing out the best buys to be quite restful. And actually, for me, it was sort of relaxing in a way. Nothing like a crowded mall full of materialistic consumers (including me!) to take my mind off of yesterday's sermon.

But the problem is, the whole shopping for back-to-school clothes seemed to fall sort of flat for me. I can't even really explain it, but I walked around in kind of a daze. I couldn't seem to focus on anything. Maybe it has to do with having just been in Mexico where there's so much poverty. I mean, they have so little and we have so much! Maybe I'm just looking at things with a whole different perspective. But suddenly I didn't feel all that interested in accumulating lots of cool stuff anymore. A lot of the clothes I'd worn last year seemed just fine to wear again this year. I mean, it's not like the styles have changed all that much anyway.

"Are you feeling okay, honey?" my mom asked with genuine concern after I turned down a great looking little top that I would've drooled over just weeks ago.

"Yeah, Mom. But I have lots of tops." Then I mentally ran down my clothing needs list and the only thing I could think of that I really, truly needed (and "needed" was questionable) was a new pair of khakis since I got a bad tear in my others that day when Beanie and Andrea and I climbed over Lynn's fence. But to be a good sport, I continued working the mall with Mom and even agreed and acted all happy when she found a really great buy on a pair of Tommy Girl jeans. But to be perfectly honest, the shopping expedition brought me no pleasure.

"Well, how about underwear and socks?" she finally pleaded, as if she thought I was turning into a mental case. So I agreed and we spent about an hour picking out what seemed an inordinate amount of "necessities."

Then we went out for a late lunch, and Mom grilled me some more about my health and everything. Was I taking my vitamins? Had I come home with any kinds of parasites or bugs that were making me act weird? Finally, she insisted on scheduling a physical for me, and to keep her happy, I agreed. And who knows, maybe I did contract some weird Mexican bug or virus. Because I must admit, I'm just not really feeling like myself today. Although it may have more to do with yesterday's hand raising than Mexico.

Tuesday. September 4 (my first day as a senior)

Well, I suppose it's kind of nice being a senior. And it was definitely cool to drive my own car to school, and I was <u>so</u> glad that Beanie was there with me. (I mean, just a couple months ago she was planning on getting her GED and becoming a mommy and everything.) But all in all, today just wasn't as great as I'd thought it would be.

I got all the classes I wanted, and it looks like I get to do the work experience program where I get off from school in the afternoon to continue working at my reception job (which I must remember to let Rita know since it was her idea in the first place). But all in all today seemed sort of anticlimactic. I'm not sure what I was expecting, though.

Several times today, I thought about the whole missionary thing again. But I still haven't told anyone. Not even Beanie. But I think I will allow myself to think about it some more. It's like I've been repressing it, as if it's this big, dark, scary thing that's going to eat me alive (which I know it's not). So now I'm telling myself, if this thing is from God, it can only be <u>good</u>. Right? And what can I possibly have to be afraid of? This rationale, I must admit, does make me feel a whole lot better. In fact, I might even talk to Pastor Tony about it. He might have some helpful thoughts to share.

Tonight I will go to bed without getting all worried and

frightened about having to become a missionary someday. Because I do know that God's love is supposed to
drive away all fear. And I think that's what I've been
feeling lately—just plain old ordinary fear.

> DEAR GOD, I'M GOING TO JUST GIVE THIS WHOLE
> MISSIONARY THING TO YOU. FIRST OF ALL, THERE
> DOESN'T SEEM TO BE MUCH I CAN DO ABOUT IT
> ANYWAY. I MEAN, I'M ONLY SEVENTEEN—WHAT AM I
> SUPPOSED TO DO? LEAVE HOME AND HITCHHIKE TO
> SOUTH AMERICA TO PREACH TO THE UNSAVED?
> AND SECOND, I KNOW THAT YOU WILL SHOW ME
> WHAT YOU WANT ME TO DO AND THEN HELP ME TO
> DO IT. AND THIRD, I KNOW THAT IF THIS THING IS
> FROM YOU, IT WILL BE GOOD AND RIGHT AND THE
> VERY BEST THING FOR ME, AND I WON'T BE
> AFRAID. SO THERE YOU HAVE IT. SHOW ME YOUR
> WAY, GOD! AMEN.

Wednesday, September 5 (a revelation?)

Tonight I went to the midweek service. I don't usually go.
I'm not even sure why not because I've discovered I like
it. But for some reason, I wanted to go tonight. I went by
myself but I sat with Stephie, who looked slightly surprised to see me there but made no comment.

It was a really fun service with lots of singing and
Pastor Tony gave a great sermon about touching the lives
of the people right around you (kind of a relief to me

when I've been thinking lately about how I might need to travel to the ends of the earth to touch people's lives). Afterwards, I went up and talked to Tony (amazingly, no one else was with him), and I told him about how his friend had made that missionary invitation, how I'd actually raised my hand, and how I'd been kind of freaking out about it ever since.

Well, Pastor Tony just smiled and said, "That's wonderful!" Now to tell the truth, I was hoping he'd say something like, "Well, Caitlin, you probably were just making an emotional response, based on the things you'd recently experienced in Mexico. Don't take it too seriously."

But no, he says, "I think it's just fantastic! And I can really envision that for you. I'm sure you'd make a terrific missionary."

"But do you think that I <u>really</u> heard God?" I asked doubtfully.

"Well, only you can know that for sure. But I don't see why not. God certainly does call some people to become missionaries. Some at even younger ages than you. I believe it could happen."

Well, my face must've revealed my heart because Tony lightened up a little then. "But think of it like this, Caitlin," he continued. "We <u>all</u> need to be missionaries. Like I said tonight, Jesus wants us to reach out to those around us. He's put us where we are for good reason. You can be a missionary without ever leaving home."

I brightened. "Yeah, you're right. I hadn't thought of it like that."

"And then—" he winked—"if God is really calling you to the foreign missions field, just think how much better prepared you'll be if you've been doing it all along at home."

I nodded halfheartedly. "Yeah, I suppose that makes sense."

He patted me on the back. "Don't worry about it. If it's God calling, nothing will bring you greater joy than answering."

I tried to smile. "I'm sure you're right. Thanks."

Well, I still don't feel any great joy about the foreign mission field, but it is a consolation to think about being a missionary right where I am. I mean, I realize how much the kids at school need God. If any place could use a missionary, it's probably Harrison High. I just don't know if I'm up to the task. Maybe I'll ask Beanie what she thinks.

Friday, September 7 (strange thing)

Well, I did tell Beanie about what Tony said (just about reaching out to our high school, NOT about the foreign missionary business!), and so we've actually been praying on our way to school this week. We're asking that God will use us to reach others and that He'll show us who needs to be reached. And Beanie starts listing off all these kids who've got problems at home or school—kids I would've called "losers" last year. But not anymore. And so I'm looking for ways to reach out to them. And it's amazing how surprised someone can be when she figures out you're for real and not just jerking her chain. I think

I've actually started a couple of new relationships.

So, guess what happens next? Jenny Lambert comes up to me right before English Lit and starts talking to me, saying how she misses me and wants to be friends again, and all this stuff. "Of course," I say. "Why not?" But at the same time I'm feeling half flattered and half confused. Like, how does this fit into my plan of being a missionary at school? I mean, because I really do like Jenny (okay, I might not have liked everything she did last year, but as a person, I think she's okay). And we actually had fun together. But how can I be a "missionary" to someone like Jenny? And furthermore, how would I explain it to Beanie? Especially when it was greatly due to my friendship with Jenny (last year) that I dumped Beanie like yesterday's news. So now I'm in a quandary and I'm not sure what to do. Other than to pray.

DEAR GOD, SHOW ME WHAT TO DO. CAN I POSSIBLY BE JENNY'S FRIEND AND REMAIN LOYAL TO BEANIE? AM I ONLY WANTING TO BE JENNY'S FRIEND BECAUSE SHE'S SO POPULAR AND IT SOUNDS LIKE FUN? AND IF I'M SUPPOSED TO BE A "MISSIONARY," I'M SURE I SHOULDN'T BE HAVING FUN IN THE FIRST PLACE. OH, PLEASE SHOW ME WHAT YOU WANT. AMEN.

TWELVE

Saturday, September 8 (a fun day)

Jenny called this morning to invite me to go out to the lake with her family. And since it was predicted to be in the nineties today, I gladly agreed. They have a really cool boat with a cabin and everything, but it's still fast enough to pull water-skiers. I've only water-skied a few times but managed to get up after only one false start where I swallowed only part of the lake. Jenny's mom packed a great picnic lunch, and all in all it was a really fun day. I always did like doing stuff with Jenny when she's away from her friends at school. It's like she's a whole different person.

And today she told me that she's getting tired of their little clique and all the superficiality. "I'm ready to be a _real_ person," she said at the end of the day as we sat on the dock with our feet dangling in the water, waiting for her dad to load up the boat. "You seem real to me, Caitlin. Not like some of my friends who can only think about one-upping somebody else."

I thanked her and considered telling her the only

reason I was real (whatever that might mean) was probably due to God, but somehow I just didn't say it.

Then she went on. "It's my senior year, and I decided not to try out for cheerleading because I'm sick and tired of playing games. I'm just going to be myself, hang with whomever I please, and just see what happens."

"I think that sounds like a great plan," I agreed. "In fact, it's pretty much what I intend to do too." I didn't mention that I'd also intended to tell everyone who would listen about God. But frankly, I wasn't doing such a hot job of that right at that moment.

We chatted some more about being real and being who we really were, and then it was time to go home. I had a fun day, and yet I felt sort of guilty when it was all said and done. Did I feel guilty for having a good time with a good friend? Or was it because of the things I didn't say? But then am I supposed to do nothing but talk about God? Or are there times just to hang out and be normal? Then again, what is "normal" anyway? For some reason I feel a little confused right now. But on the other hand, I'm tired and don't really want to think about it too hard.

Friday, September 14 (finding normal)

To tell the truth, I don't really feel like writing in my diary much today. The only reason I'm writing is because it's been several days, and I've got a few minutes to kill. But it's not like I haven't been writing anything; I actually wrote a long letter to Josh just yesterday. And besides,

I've been busy working after school, and then I've been doing a lot with Jenny lately too. We're becoming pretty good friends.

I've tried to include Beanie, like inviting her to eat lunch together and stuff. And I think Jenny actually likes her. But Beanie seems to want to distance herself, like she looks down on Jenny or something. Now, that bugs me a lot, because I think just because Jenny's been "popular" doesn't mean that God doesn't want us to hang with her, does it? I mean, does God like the loser types better than the popular types? I don't think so. And that might not even be what Beanie is thinking. I'm not totally sure. In fact, I haven't even talked to Beanie for a couple of days now. Maybe <u>that's</u> what's bugging her. But then, it's a two-way street—she can make the move to talk to me just as easily as I can to her.

Anyway, I think I've written just about enough for now. Besides, Jenny's going to be here soon. I'm not sure what we're doing tonight, but I'm sure it'll be fun. And I have to admit, I'm enjoying just being a <u>normal seventeen-year-old girl</u> again. And I'm trying not to think too much about heavy things these days. I had my physical and the doctor told my mom that maybe the trip to Mexico had caused me to suffer stress, or perhaps I'd been having a little culture shock. Anyway, he told me to just take it easy. And that's just what I've been doing. So, is there anything wrong with that?

Wednesday, September 19 (accusations)

I'm not going to apologize for not writing in my diary every day. I'm just not going to do it. I'm tired of apologizing, and besides I've been pretty busy lately and life's been fun. Jenny and I are having a great time being seniors; we just do whatever we want, hang with whomever we want, and we don't worry about what anyone thinks. It's great! And we do try to include Beanie, really we do! And occasionally she actually joins in, but usually she doesn't. I'm not even sure why, but I think she may be jealous of Jenny. Still, I do lots of stuff with Beanie (I certainly have NOT dumped her), but I figure there's room in my life for more than just one friend. (Although I do consider Beanie to be my best friend and have told her as much, but I doubt she completely believes me.) And I still consider Andrea to be a good friend too, but since she goes to another school, it's more natural not to hang together so much. What's wrong with having a variety of friends anyway?

But that's not how Beanie sees it. And I guess it should come as no surprise when she calls me up tonight and says some pretty mean things. At least I think they're mean. She says she's just trying (in her words) to speak the truth in love. So she proceeds to tell me how she went to church tonight and Pastor Tony was preaching on this very subject, and now she feels like she's supposed to come home, call me up, and tell me all about it. "Thanks anyway," I tell her, "but if I'd wanted to hear Tony's sermon, I would've gone to church myself."

Well, talk about opening a can of worms. She then feels it's her Christian responsibility to tell me that she's "worried about _my_ spiritual condition." Those were _her_ words! And I'm wondering, who is she to worry about _my_ condition? I mean, this is the girl who got herself pregnant last year, was nearly suicidal, and pretty much a great, big mess. But do I mention these uncomfortable subjects? No way! But as a result, Beanie just launches into this little sermonette about how she used to look up to me in spiritual things, but now she thinks I'm just throwing everything away in order to be Jenny Lambert's best friend.

"I am _not_ Jenny's best friend!" I shoot back at her. "We're just good friends. And besides, I thought you and I were trying to reach out to people at Harrison—"

"Have you told her about Jesus, Caitlin?"

I resent the question and don't even want to answer, but I give it a try. "You know there's more than one way to share something with someone," I begin, feeling a little hopeless. "Maybe I want to build a friendship with her first, and then I can share later."

"Well, that's perfectly fine, Caitlin, but I'm just wondering who's influencing whom here? Every day, I see you starting to act more and more like Jenny and less and less like yourself. It seems like you just don't care about the same things anymore. And I can't figure it out. I mean, would you just throw away everything God has done for you to be friends with Jenny Lambert?"

Now I know Beanie really does care about me (we've been through too much together to believe anything else), but the tone of her voice is getting pretty sharp, and she sounds genuinely mad. And frankly she's really hurting my feelings. But I don't tell her that. I only tell her she's being totally ridiculous and that I'm sorry she feels this way. There seems to be little else to say, and we both hang up. And now I feel absolutely lousy.

But the truth is, this really doesn't have all that much to do with Jenny Lambert. And no, I wouldn't throw God away for Jenny, or anyone for that matter. At least, I hope not. But I do think I might be using Jenny's friendship as a distraction maybe (not that I'm using Jenny because I do believe we are friends, really and truly). But spending time with her might be sort of an escape from something I don't quite want to face just yet.

Okay, maybe I know exactly what it is that I'm trying to escape, but I don't want to admit it. You see, it's hard to put these feelings down into words. I'm not ready to see them in bold black ink just yet.

So maybe I can deal with this tomorrow.

Friday, September 21 (apologies and stuff)

Today (after a day of silent treatment times two yesterday) Beanie made the first move and apologized to me. I told her I was sorry too, but that I was confused about some things (I didn't go into detail). But we ended up hugging and crying. And Jenny watched the whole thing with amusement, then told us that she loved how "real" we were, then invited us to go to the football game with her tonight. To my amazed wonder, Beanie agreed to come and was even a good sport the whole time. We all ended up laughing and joking and having a fun time.

After the game, we went out for pizza. A lot of kids were there and it was pretty wild and messy. And afterwards, Beanie and I talked Jenny into hanging around and helping to clean up the mess (Beanie's idea, although I agreed it was a good one). At first, Jenny thought we were joking, but then I pointed out the couple who owned the place looked harried and tired and would probably appreciate it. So then she just jumped right in. Well, just as we were finishing up, the guy came up and commented on what nice young ladies we were, to which Beanie added, "It's only because of Jesus in us." And I nodded, not really wanting to give a public testimony but not wanting to put Beanie off again either.

Then the guy says, "Oh, that's nice. You're Christian girls then?"

To which Jenny answers proudly, "Just them, not me."

The guy chuckles and picks up a loaded tray. "Well, you two will have to get to work on your friend then."

I feel kind of embarrassed, but Jenny just laughs. "It's okay that you two are Christians," she says somewhat patronizingly, "we can still be friends."

Well, I suppose that's a start.

Sunday, September 23 (suspicions begin)

After church today, Beanie and Andrea and I went to the mall. And while we were getting a snack, Beanie ups and says, "I think Jenny Lambert is anorexic."

Now let me tell you, I'm already getting pretty defensive when it comes to Jenny, but this comment totally throws me for a loop. "What are you talking about?" I ask incredulously.

"I just think she is."

"Beanie, I thought you were starting to like her—"

"This has nothing to do with that," she declares as Andrea watches with curious interest.

"But why are you saying that?" I just roll my eyes and keep from mentioning anything about how Beanie put on a little weight with her pregnancy, which still hasn't come off. "Is it just because Jenny's thin?"

"No, it's more than that. Open your eyes, Cate."

Now I'm trying not to be offended. "Beanie, you're a Christian, and you know we're not supposed to judge others. But here you go, coming down on Jenny again. I don't think it's right."

"Yeah," agrees Andrea, who's never even met Jenny.

Beanie holds up her hands defensively. "Look," she begins in a softer tone. "The only reason I'm mentioning it at all is because I'm concerned. And I think you're one of her best friends now, Cate. I just thought you should be aware is all."

"Aware of what?" I snap.

"That she could have anorexia nervosa, a condition that commonly affects teenage girls who—"

"Enough!" I slam my soda cup down. "I don't need a textbook explanation on anorexia, Beanie, I <u>know</u> what it is. Good grief, I've even been accused of having it myself, which is totally ridiculous."

"Sorry, but you were acting so dense, I wasn't sure."

Now to my relief, Andrea breaks in. "So, Beanie, tell us why you're so sure that Jenny is anorexic."

"Well, first of all, have you ever seen her eat anything?"

I considered this. I mean, I've shared lots of meals with Jenny. But the more I thought about it, the more I wondered if I'd ever actually seen her consume a piece of food. She'd fiddle with food and talk and joke a lot. "I've seen her drink soda," I offer.

"Yeah," agrees Beanie. "Diet soda."

"Lots of people drink diet soda."

"I do," says Andrea helpfully.

"Yeah, but you're having a giant pretzel with it. Jenny doesn't eat real food."

"That's crazy." I shake my head in disbelief. "Jenny's a perfectly normal girl. She's not anorexic."

"Well, I didn't expect you to believe me," says Beanie, clearly dismayed.

"It's not that I don't," I say. "But I think you're being too hard on her."

She shrugs. "I just thought since you're her friend, you might want to keep your eyes open, just in case you can be of any help."

"Okay," I say with reluctance. "I'll keep this in mind."

Now Beanie's planted this seed of suspicion in my head against Jenny, and I suppose for the next few days

I'll be watching her to make sure that she's eating right.
Oh, brother!

THIRTEEN

Tuesday, September 25 (concerns)

Okay, now I'm thinking Beanie is right on target about Jenny. I've watched her closely for two days and haven't seen her consume a single bite of food. Oh, she's very clever about it, never draws attention to the fact she's not eating, and even makes comments about the food. But I'm afraid Beanie's right—Jenny's not eating. And today the three of us were sitting outside enjoying the last days of summer (actually it's fall, but the weather is still good) and I noticed that Jenny's not just thin, she's skinny as a stick. I even mentioned it and she just said, "No way, you're the one who's skinny, Caitlin." I tried to show her that she was lots skinnier, but she just kept laughing and denying it. Beanie gave me a look that said, see. And I didn't know what to do. Now I feel pretty worried about Jenny. I mean, people can die from anorexia, and the worst part is they have a real tough time admitting that they have it. I've heard stories where girls are nothing but skin and bones but still see themselves as fat. I don't want that to happen to

Jenny. But I don't know what to say or do.

And now I've got another admission to make. I haven't been praying a whole lot lately. I guess I've been sort of afraid. Not of God, exactly. But maybe of what I think He's telling me to do. And yet, I really want to pray for Jenny. But I'm thinking, how can I go to God, begging Him to help Jenny when I'm not even going to Him to ask for help for myself.

Basically, I'm feeling just about as down as I've ever felt in the last year or so. Okay, maybe I'm not borderline suicidal (like the first time Josh broke my heart) but that was before I had God. But what worries me now is, what if I've turned my back on God (like Beanie had suggested I was doing a week or so ago)? I mean, I went to church, and I've even read my Bible a few times, but something in me is shut down. And it scares me. A lot.

So as worried as I am about my friend Jenny, I guess I'm even more worried about myself. The truth is, I don't know if I can even live without God in my life anymore. And right now, my heart feels like there's a great, big boulder sitting on it. Oh, why have I allowed myself to reach this place where I'm even asking these questions? And where do I go for the answers?

Wednesday, September 26 (truth)

I was so bummed out at school today that Beanie and Jenny both kept asking me what was wrong. To which I could not even find the words to answer. Finally, I just went home early on the pretense of being sick. (I even

called Rita and told her I wouldn't be in.) And I believe I
am sick. But in my spirit. And I suppose if one is sick in her
spirit for long, it can't help but affect her body. But for
now it's just in my spirit. And I know it's time for Caitlin
Renee O'Conner to do some honest to goodness soul-
searching. So that's exactly what I plan to do. I can't
keep living like this, pretending to be what I'm not, not
knowing what I am, running from God, or acting like I don't
care. I just can't do it anymore!

DEAR GOD, I NEED YOUR HELP—DESPERATELY! I
KNOW I'VE BEEN AVOIDING YOU. AND I'M TRULY
SORRY. I REALIZE THAT I NEED YOU MORE THAN
EVER BEFORE. BUT I CONFESS THAT I'M AFRAID.
I'M AFRAID YOU'VE ASKED ME TO DO SOMETHING I
CANNOT DO. IT'S NOT THAT I DON'T WANT TO BE
A MISSIONARY FOR YOU, GOD. IT'S JUST THAT I'M
AFRAID I CAN'T DO IT—NOT UP TO THE TASK. I
MEAN, TWO WEEKS IN MEXICO IS ONE THING, BUT A
LIFETIME COMMITMENT TO SERVING YOU AS A
MISSIONARY IS SOMETHING ELSE ALTOGETHER. I
KNOW I MUST BE A BIG DISAPPOINTMENT TO YOU,
AND FOR THAT I'M SORRY. PLEASE HELP ME. AMEN.

Thursday, September 27 (encouragement)

I'm feeling a little better today. This morning, Beanie
grilled me on the way to school, and I finally ended up
just pouring out the whole missionary story. And she was so

relieved. "Oh, Cate," she gushed happily. "This is such a relief. I thought maybe something really serious was wrong."

"But this is serious," I said as I pulled into the student parking lot. "It feels as if my faith is hanging in the balance."

"That's not how I see it." She thought for a moment. "To me, it just seems like God is calling you to a deeper level of faith and you're struggling with it."

I nodded. "Yeah, that's kind of how it seems. But ever since that mission thing happened, it feels like I'm pulling away from God." I blinked back tears. "But I've just come to realize that I can't do that. I cannot live like that, Beanie. It's like there's no going back for me."

She reached over and laid a comforting hand on my arm. "It's going to be okay, Cate. I just know it, inside my heart. Everything is going to turn out just fine."

"I wish I felt as sure as you do." Then it was time to head to class. But her words were encouraging. And when I saw Jenny later, she asked if I was feeling better and I said "a little," but didn't go into any detail.

Then at lunch, Beanie came to sit with Jenny and me and she asked how my spiritual trial was going (well, not in those words, but plainly enough as to get Jenny's curiosity).

"What's that all about?" asked Jenny as she pretended to chew on a carrot stick. (And I'm thinking, Just go ahead and eat it; it's only a carrot stick for Pete's sake!)

But instead I actually answered her, surprising even myself. "You know what you've been saying about being real, Jenny? Well, I haven't been real. Not with myself or you, and worst of all to God."

Well, she just sort of blinked, then asked me what I meant. And I tried to explain how I felt like I'd turned my back on God lately (not mentioning the missions thing, which I'm sure she would never in a million years understand!), but how I'd become progressively more miserable, and finally reached the point where I couldn't go on. "So you see, Jenny, I'm a Christian. And there's nothing more important to me than God. And if you don't want to hang with me because of that, it's fine." I could see that last line wasn't quite making sense, so I tried to soften it a little. "What I mean is, I am going to be who I am no matter what anyone else thinks. And I'd like to still be friends, but I've figured out that I need God more than I need even the best of friends."

She kind of laughed then said, "Gee, Cate, I never thought I was making you choose between me and God."

I smiled. "I know. It was me who was having the problem. Actually, I think I was trying to distract myself more than anything." Then I told her all about the trip to Mexico and how I'd really become concerned about the kids.

"I think that's cool," she said with genuine enthusiasm.

"But the thing is," I went on, "I even started feeling like I'd turned my back on the kids. And that was just killing me."

"Oh, I think I'm beginning to get the picture."

Finally Beanie jumped in. "Yeah, even Josh Miller has gotten really concerned about the kids down there."

"Josh?" Jenny's eyes flashed.

"Yeah. He went on the mission too," said Beanie, glancing at me nervously, as if she'd said something wrong.

"Josh had been attending our church youth group," I quickly explained. "And he went with us to Mexico."

Jenny frowned. "And so are you and Josh, you know, going out now?"

I laughed. "Not at all. We're just friends, and we both know it."

"Oh." Then she laughed. "Not that I'd care. I mean, that was a lifetime ago."

"I know. But Josh has really changed since then."

She kind of rolled her eyes. "I'll bet."

We talked a little more about the Mexico trip, then Jenny said she wouldn't mind doing something like that someday. "I think it's great to help kids like that." So I told her about my campaign to raise money for food, and she asked if she could help too.

"Of course. I'd love for you to help."

And suddenly everything was starting to feel almost like it had before. Well, almost. I still have some things to resolve between God and me. But now I don't feel quite so anxious as I did yesterday. Somehow the things that happened today have made me feel a new confidence. Beanie claims it's because she's been really praying for me. And I'm sure that's a big part of it. But I think there's something more going on here too. I think it's mostly up to me to figure this thing out. The best part is, now I don't feel like I'm afraid to do it!

Sunday, September 30 (back on track)

Today at youth group, Greg read an excerpt from "The Journals of Jim Elliot," which is the actual journal of a man named Jim Elliot who was a missionary in Ecuador about fifty years ago or so. Anyway, it was this really cool entry about how he wanted to give his all for God and to trust Him for everything, but it was so honestly written! I couldn't believe it had been written so long ago by some pioneer missionary, because this guy sounded like someone who could be a good friend. And Greg said he wasn't really that old at the time (I think he was in his twenties).

Then Greg closes the book and tells us how not long after those words were written, Jim and his buddy were killed by some of the natives they were trying to reach for God. Now I suppose this sounds kind of gruesome and everything (and it really was a tragedy), but for some reason this story of some missionaries being literally martyred for their faith just totally got to me. But not in a sad or negative way. I mean, suddenly I'm thinking, it would be an honor to die for God.

And okay, I'll admit that just days ago I was running from God (or at least I thought I was), but maybe I was just running from myself and thinking I wasn't up to doing whatever it was that God was calling me to do. But suddenly I'm not worried about any of that anymore. And I'm thinking that, sure, I could go serve God as a mission-ary, and I could even die if need be. Just like that. Pretty weird, huh?

But the truth is, I would rather live like that (sold out for God) than the way I've been living these past few weeks. I'd rather know that I totally belong to God and that He's in control of my life than to feel like I'm running or hiding or whatever. Because God's way is better. I just know it. And now that I've reached this place, I feel so free and happy and secure. And now I realize that it's the only place I want to be.

So then after telling us about this missionary, Greg reads a quote of his which I wrote down and am now going to put in my diary as well as on my wall. It goes like this:

He is no fool who gives what he cannot keep to gain what he cannot lose. Jim Elliot

And that just about sums it up for me. I think I was trying to hang on to something—I'm not even sure exactly what, but I was hanging on to it for dear life—and it was killing me! Now I feel like whatever it was (whether it was me, my life, my choices, whatever) that I have let it go. Now I'm just hanging on to God, and I feel more alive and more fulfilled and just plain happier than ever. And, ah, what a huge relief it is!

And you know what's really cool? I've started thinking

about those kids at the dump again and praying for them more than ever. I can even imagine going down there to live and to work full time. I mean, I'm dreaming up ways that I might get the funds together to have a building built with a kitchen and day care facilities and laundry and who knows what else!

Okay, I know I'm only seventeen and not even out of high school yet, but I can dream, can't I? And I can pray! Let me tell you, this is a whole lot better than running the other way!

FOURTEEN

Wednesday, October 3 (confrontation)

Today at lunch, I just couldn't stand it anymore. Try as I might, I could NOT keep my eyes off Jenny
as she just picked and picked and PICKED at her tossed
green salad, while casually sipping from her 32-ounce Diet
Coke. And finally, to my later and extreme embarrassment, the words just blurted out of me.

"Just eat the stupid salad, Jenny!"

She looked up at me in surprise, then calmly said,
"What's up with that little comment?" Still slightly
shocked at my own unexpected outburst, I almost
backed down, but then something came over me as I
noticed (not for the first time) her tiny, bony wrists, and I
knew I could no longer just sit by and say nothing. So I
continued. "Jenny, I know what's going on with you."

Her eyes narrowed a little. "What do you mean?"

"I mean I know you might have an eating disorder,
okay? It's nothing to feel bad or guilty about, and you
don't need to try to cover it up, but I really think you
should get some help."

She just stared at me for a long moment, then stood and made her move to leave the table.

"Please don't go, Jenny," I pleaded, suddenly feeling stupid and guilty over my abrupt confrontation. "You know I'm your friend and that I really care about you." I glanced around the noisy cafeteria, thinking where was Beanie when you need her? Usually she joined us for lunch these days, and I felt pretty certain she'd have something informative and helpful to say. Unfortunately, I could think of neither.

"Well, if you really do care about me, Cate, then maybe you shouldn't say mean things like that." She sat back down.

"I'm just worried about your health, Jen. Really."

"I'm perfectly fine, thank you very much."

"Okay, then tell me, when did you last eat?"

She looked me in the eye with defiance. "Now."

"You haven't actually eaten one single bite."

"So you're counting my bites now?"

"No, that's not it. I just know what's going on with you. Can't you see you're getting thinner and thinner? And I know that can't be good. Have you seen a doctor or anything?"

She looked down at her neatly rearranged salad: tomatoes and cucumbers on one side, lettuce on the other, dressing "on the side" and still on the side. "Don't worry so much, Caitlin, I'm fine, really I am. You're just imagining things."

"No," I said with fresh conviction. "I'm not imagining

anything. How much do you weigh right now, Jenny?"

She shrugged.

"I know that you know. You probably weighed yourself this morning."

She still didn't answer.

"Jenny," I pleaded, "I'm your friend; I want to help."

Then she looked at me evenly then said, "You can't."

Well, as weak as it was, it did seem an admission of sorts. "Then who can?"

"I don't know."

"But do you realize that if you keep this up, you could seriously harm yourself or even die?"

Her eyes looked slightly frightened now. "I know that."

"But..." I struggled for words. "Is that what you want?"

Eyes downcast, she slowly shook her head.

"So what are you going to do about it?"

"I don't know."

"Jenny, do your parents know what's going on?"

She kind of laughed at this. "Dad's too busy to notice much of anything, and Mom thinks I'm just fashionably thin. Did you know I can wear size one jeans now?"

I remembered the day at the lake about a month ago. Jenny had never removed her T-shirt from over her swimsuit. And even now she wore a baggy sweater over loose jeans. A great cover-up.

"You've got to let them know, Jen."

She took in a deep breath. "I can't."

I reached over and put my hand on her arm. "But Jenny, can you at least admit that you do have a problem?"

Without looking up, her head moved up and down, just barely, and I sighed in relief. "Will you let me help you then?"

"I don't know how you can help, Cate. I mean, it's just not that simple. It's like, I keep telling myself I'll start eating again, but somehow I just can't do it. I try and try. And no matter what I do, I can't."

Once again, I asked, "Jenny, will you let me help?"

"Thanks for caring, Cate, but it's my problem and I don't know what you can possibly do to change anything."

"I don't know either, but I want to try. And just so you'll know, I've been praying for you. And so has Beanie."

She made a little half smile, then spoke in a somewhat condescending tone. "Do you really think that makes any difference, Caitlin? I mean, if I can't help myself, then why would God want to help me? And the truth is, I'm not so sure that I even believe in God."

Well, I couldn't help myself now (or maybe it was a God-thing), but I just boldly said, "You know, Jenny, for someone who doesn't believe in God, you're sure playing awfully close to the line where you just might find out whether He's real or not."

That seemed to get to her, and I noticed her eyes getting watery now. "Yeah, I suppose you could be right."

By then the second bell had rung and we had to dash to class, but I paused for a split second to look her in the eye. "Jenny, I intend on sticking by you through this. Is that okay?"

She kind of shrugged again. "Sure, whatever."

I didn't see her again today. But right after work, I came home and called Beanie and told her all about everything I'd said, and I asked if she had any suggestions. And without missing a beat she told me I should call Jenny's mom and tell her all about this.

"But that feels like I'm ratting on Jenny."

"If you saw a friend holding a gun to her head, would you call someone for help?"

"Well, that's different."

"Just quicker is all. But listen, Caitlin, just do Jenny and her parents a great, big favor and tell them what's up."

"But what if Jenny gets mad at me?"

"She probably will."

"But I think she needs me right now, Beanie. I don't want to blow her trust. I'm probably her closest friend at the moment; you know how she doesn't hang with any of her old friends anymore. And, speaking of friends, I sure wish you'd been around at lunchtime. I really could've used some backup."

"Sorry, I had to do some research on the Net in the library. But I'll be around tomorrow. In the meantime, just tell her parents what's up."

"I'll pray about it."

"Well, I suppose that's a start."

After I hung up, I _did_ pray. As I did, an idea occurred to me. I decided I could write an anonymous letter. And if Jenny eventually guessed it was me, then I'd have to just live with it. But certainly that's better than doing

nothing. I sat at my computer and typed out what I
hoped sounded like a mature letter written by a concerned adult (like a teacher or something). I even went
online and printed off a couple of good articles about
anorexia nervosa that I included in the letter. And
thanks to my job, I know how to print addresses on
envelopes by computer, so the whole thing looks pretty
slick, if I do say so myself, and it's all sealed and
stamped and ready to go first thing in the morning.

But before I go to bed, I will say another prayer for
Jenny (I've been praying for her health on and off
throughout the day), but now I plan to pray for her spiritual condition—her heart. Ultimately that's the most
important part anyway.

Thursday, October 4 (news from afar)

Jenny avoided me today, and I didn't see her anywhere
at lunchtime. Part of me was slightly relieved, afraid
that I'd say something to give away what I'd done last
night. I really hope she never discovers that I'm the one
who wrote that letter. But on the other hand, I did miss
seeing her and I'm desperately worried about her condition (especially after reading that stuff from the
anorexia Web site last night).

On a happier note, I got a nice letter from Josh today,
almost three pages long (double-spaced, of course). I think
he's feeling a little overwhelmed by college. Not quite as
easy as high school, I suspect. But it was great to hear
he's still thinking about God and taking his faith seri-

ously. He's even gotten involved in an early morning Bible study group, and he sent me a twenty-dollar bill to add to the Mexico garbage dump kids' fund. (I've got to come up with a proper name for this thing!) Maybe an acronym like FOOD (Feeding Orphans On the Dumpsite). Well, I guess I better give that one some more careful thought. Besides, the kids aren't really orphans, they just have some pretty hopeless parents.

Anyway, I decided to write back to Josh tonight, so I guess I'll have to cut my diary entry a little shorter than usual.

Friday, October 5 (concerns)

Jenny wasn't at school today, and I guess I'm feeling pretty worried that she might be sick as a result of her not eating. And yes, I suppose I feel a little guilty too because I'm sure her mom got my letter by now, and I wonder what will happen next. I mean, it's not like I'm going to get her into trouble or anything like that (actually I'd only wanted to spare her from some really <u>serious</u> troubles). But to be honest, this whole thing is getting to me. I mean, it's all I could think about today. And it's not that I haven't been praying for her, because <u>I have</u>. But for some reason I'm feeling sort of responsible for her. Like for one thing, I'm thinking, I've been her best friend during these past few weeks, I probably should've noticed something was wrong way sooner than this. I mean, it took Beanie harping at me about it before I actually noticed anything suspicious. And even then I wasn't totally convinced she had anorexia.

Okay, I know it's not my personal fault that Jenny does-n't eat food. I mean, after all, I _did_ read those articles I sent to her mom, and I know it's a pretty complicated problem that a person mostly brings upon herself. Like if a girl feels she doesn't have all that much control over what happens in her life, she might decide to focus her energy inward (onto her body) by choosing to deprive her-self of food. Because for some reason, following a strict diet gives that girl this weird sense of control and then when she consequently loses weight she feels all empow-ered by it.

But, to be honest, this doesn't really make a whole lot of sense to me. I mean, how could depriving yourself of food make you feel powerful? It would only make me feel hungry and grumpy and totally frustrated.

I'll admit I sort of get the part about girls wanting to be "ultrathin" because of all the models and media and stuff. And it does seem like almost every girl I know wor-ries about her weight now and then (some to the point of obnoxious obsession!), and I've even had friends give me a bad time because I can pretty much eat whatever I want without freaking about my weight too much. (But then my mom's like that too and according to her we have "slim genes," which is fortunate because, personally, it's just one less thing to worry about.) But I do under-stand how this focus on thinness and weight is a national compulsion with teenage girls. And according to one article I read, girls who have anorexia get this kind of euphoric high when they get on the scales and see they've lost another pound. They say it's almost like taking a happy pill or something. And it makes them feel like they're in control of their lives and like they're succeeding at something. Which seems totally weird if you ask me. I mean, these girls (by the way, some guys get it too) are succeeding at starving their bodies until they have no energy, and they can no longer eat any kind of food. Then their hair falls out, and their periods stop, their teeth go bad, their bones get weak, and the list gets worse. I mean, who (in her right mind) would willingly invite all these kinds of ailments into her life? Apparently Jenny. I just don't get it. Big sigh...

According to one psychiatrist online, a lot of these girls have some things in common. One thing is that they tend to put too much pressure on themselves, I think like an overachiever. (I learned that term in psychology—those are people who work incredibly hard to succeed; they are also called Type A personalities, which Jenny probably is.) And girls with anorexia also tend to be really good students (like Jenny) and often well liked and popular (like Jenny) and perfectionists (like Jenny!). I mean, you should see her room—it's immaculate! Not only is it decorated perfectly, but every single thing is always in its place. In fact, her room is so neat I sometimes wonder how she can even stand it. Sometimes I want to go in there and just mess things up a little so I can relax and feel comfortable. But of course I don't. Although, I'll confess to having moved her hairbrush from its regular spot on her dresser once. But within mere minutes, she had put it right back in place without saying a word. At the time, I wondered: What's up with that? Now, I think I know.

But the thing is, I like Jenny so much that I've tried to overlook these little idiosyncrasies (another psychology class word that means "our unique differences"). And I suppose I thought I might try to learn a thing or two from her about neatness and organization. Although I certainly do NOT want to become obsessed with it. We were studying OCD in my psychology class this week (that stands for obsessive compulsive disorder), and I guess I'm wondering if Jenny might not have something like that too. Although it's hard to say. That whole anorexia thing might be her only problem. And let me tell you, it's a pretty big one!

This whole biz is worrying me quite a lot these days. But at least I think her mom is on the up-and-up now. And Beanie and I have both been really praying for Jen, and even Aunt Steph is praying for her. Beanie told her all about it, and I guess Steph (who didn't inherit those same "slim genes") came pretty close to being anorexic herself, just after she got out of high school, but she told Beanie it was a piece of cherry cheesecake that finally cured her and turned her around. Maybe we should try that with Jenny, although I think something chocolate might work better. Last year she used to just love chocolate.

I'd really like to call her right now and see what's up, but at the same time I'm a little worried she might have figured out somehow that I'm the one who ratted on her about this whole thing. Okay, according to Beanie, it wasn't ratting. Beanie keeps saying I did her a huge life-saving favor and that she'll never guess it was me. But just the same I feel pretty guilty.

FIFTEEN

Saturday, October 6 (chocolate cheesecake falls short)

Today I called and invited Jenny to go to the
mall (thinking I'd try to get her to eat something there),
but she said she wasn't feeling too well and that's why
she'd missed school yesterday. I asked her if it had anything to do with her not eating and she got a little irate.
"You know, I'm getting a little fed up with all this talk
about anorexia, Caitlin. I've just got a cold is all. Is it
okay for a person to catch a silly little cold these days?
Or do you want to ship me off to the psycho ward too?"

"The psycho ward?"

"Yeah, some moronic teacher, or maybe it's that stupid counselor Ms. Fieldstone, sent my mom this totally
ridiculous letter telling her that I may be anorexic. And
now my mom's all freaked and ready to check me into
the loony bin."

"Oh no!"

"Yeah, tell me about it. She put in a call to some stupid shrink friend of hers at West Haven."

"You're kidding?" Guilt, guilt, guilt...big-time guilt.

"I wish. My mom's already made me stand on the scales, which sent her straight into hysterics, then she actually tried to force-feed me, and she's now saying I cannot leave this house without eating something. I feel like I'm in prison." I heard her voice choke. "I just don't know why this is happening to me, Cate."

Well, I hardly need to say that I'm feeling absolutely horrible by then. Like this whole anorexia thing was totally my fault, and how could I possibly stop whatever I'd set into motion with her mother. "Uh, is there anything I can do to help?" I asked lamely.

She just groaned. "No one can help me, no one but me. And I don't even know what I can do to change."

"Do you want me to come over?"

She paused then said, "Sure, if you want to. But I'll warn you, my mom is just totally wigging out on me. I can't be responsible for anything she might say or do."

I tried to laugh. "That's okay. Parents are like that."

So, remembering what Aunt Steph said, I stopped by Celeste's Bakery and got two fat slices of their "to die for" chocolate cheesecake and then headed over to Jenny's.

She acted all excited about the cheesecake (I'm sure to impress her mom) and made a big production of putting them on plates and getting forks and napkins, and then we sat down at the breakfast bar to eat them.

And I have to give Jenny credit, she did put a couple of
bites into her mouth. But then she started to gag.
Literally gag! And she had to run to the bathroom, and I
felt so bad for her I couldn't even eat the rest of my
cheesecake. And believe me, it really was the ultimate
in chocolate cheesecake!

Well, the whole time this was going on, her mom kept
flitting around the kitchen, all nervouslike, and saying
stupid little things (that I don't think were making Jenny
feel one bit better!) and then she just burst into tears.

So Jenny and I went to the pool room and tried to play
a game of pool, but I could tell she was really weak and
everything, so I finally convinced her to just sit down and
rest. And then she started to cry.

"I don't know what to do," she sobbed. "I don't want to
go to West Haven—I don't want to be analyzed by a
bunch of shrinks or take a lot of stupid pills—and I know
they'll put a feeding tube in me if I don't eat—and I just
can't stand to think of that."

I leaned over and hugged her and she continued to
cry, really pitifully—just like a hopeless little kid. And I
felt so totally bad. I didn't know what to say or do or
anything.

But then I did something that completely surprised
me. Something I've never done before (and don't know if I
could ever even do again). All I can say is that it must've
been a God-thing. Because without even thinking it
through, or asking if it was okay, I just started to pray for
her, right out loud! I can't even remember exactly what I

said when I prayed. I mean, I think I basically prayed for normal stuff like her being able to eat again, and also that she'd ask God to help her, and even that she'd be healed from this horrible illness. Stuff like that. But anyway, by the time I finished praying, she had stopped crying and was sitting up and studying me carefully. And then (to my surprise) she said thanks and that she felt better.

Well, she seemed pretty much exhausted to me, and I suppose I felt a little embarrassed (why is that?), so I suggested maybe she'd like to rest some, and then I left. But I prayed for her some more as I drove home.

I called her just a little while ago to see how she's doing, but her mom answered and said she'd gone to bed. I asked Mrs. Lambert if she thought Jenny might like to go to church with me tomorrow, and she said she'd let her know I'd invited her. But something about the way she said it suggested that she really didn't want Jenny to go with me. So then I asked how she thought Jenny was doing.

"Don't worry about Jenny," she said kind of abruptly (as if I have no involvement in this thing at all). "She's had some problems, but we're getting her the very best of help. Everything is under control now."

"Is there anything I can do?"

"No. Just let her friends know that she's going to be fine. And she should be back at school in no time."

"Does this mean she's going to West Haven?"

Mrs. Lambert cleared her throat. "I don't know how

much Jenny has told you, Caitlin, but her father and I would greatly appreciate your confidentiality in this matter. This isn't the sort of thing we want circulating all over town."

Well, I felt as if I'd been slapped, but I managed to conceal my hurt. "Of course," I agreed. "Jenny is my friend. I just want for her to get better."

"That's what we want too. Thank you for calling. I'll let Jenny know."

I hung up and just stared at the phone. <u>They were taking her to West Haven</u>. Poor, poor Jenny. Then Mrs. Lambert's words echoed in my mind: "Everything's under control..." and that's when I began to cry.

Despite my "promise" not to tell anyone, I called Beanie (swearing her to absolute secrecy) and asked her to keep praying for Jenny. "I think her mom is part of the problem," I explained. "It seems like she really tries to control Jenny. And according to some things I've read, anorexia is all about control."

"Well, then maybe she'll be better off at a place like West Haven," said Beanie with her ever-practical rationale.

"But it's just what she didn't want."

"Sometimes we don't know what we really want."

"I suppose." I sighed deeply. "I just feel like a lot of this is my fault."

"Caitlin," she began in what sounded like her I'm-about-to-give-you-a-lecture voice. "You can't take care of everyone, you know. I mean, I realize how you have this very compassionate and caring nature, and a tendency to get pretty involved in other people's lives. But you need to understand that everything is NOT your personal fault or responsibility. People make their own choices. You've got to accept that you just can't help every single person you meet. And you certainly can't feed every hungry kid on the planet either, no matter how badly you want to. Remember, you're just one person and you can only do so much."

"I know. But God is bigger than that. I believe He can do all those things."

"Then let Him."

I wasn't totally sure what she meant by that but felt too emotionally wrung out to figure it all out anyway. So I thanked her for her (what I assumed was) well-meant, albeit harsh, advice and told her I'd see her at church tomorrow.

Wednesday, October 10 (okay, so no one's perfect)

Today in psychology class we learned about codependent personalities and now I'm afraid I might actually be one— and let me tell you, it's not a pretty picture. But the good news is this personality disorder is preventable and curable, and I'm thinking if I nip it in the bud (not to mention going to God for help) I might be able to beat it. So what is codependent? At first I just thought it meant someone who depends on others too much, and I suppose that's partially right. But it's more like someone who thinks that they need to take care of everyone else and fix everything else to the point where their whole identity is tied up in caring and worrying about others. Sound familiar? And eventually they neglect themselves so much that they have no joy in living, and then they tend to just make everyone around them miserable with their guilt trips and meddling.

Well, let me tell you, that's NOT what I want for my life. Not at all. No sireee! Now I'm trying to understand the difference between a person who is just naturally helpful and caring and the one who's truly a codependent. I'm just not sure exactly where I draw that line in myself. And I must admit that over just the last year, I've made myself almost sick with worry about others from time to time. I mean, I can list the people I've been concerned for on TWO hands. To start with there was my mom and dad and their marriage problems, and before Christmas it was Aunt Steph, then Beanie with her pregnancy, Josh just because he's Josh, and for a while I was worried about Andrea, and then Zach with his drug problems, and lately it's been Jenny. And this whole thing is starting to worry me a lot! It's like I can see an unhealthy pattern here. So I figure I better let God straighten me out before I go out and do something really stupid, like marry a drug addict or alcoholic (lots of codependents do that sort of thing!).

DEAR GOD, PLEASE SHOW ME THE DIFFERENCE BETWEEN REALLY HELPING SOMEONE THE RIGHT WAY AND BEING CODEPENDENT. I THINK IF MY CARING

AND LOVE COMES FROM YOU, I'LL BE OKAY. BUT I'M
JUST NOT SURE HOW TO KNOW THE DIFFERENCE.
PLEASE SHOW ME HOW TO LIVE MY LIFE IN A
HEALTHY WAY THAT IS PLEASING TO YOU. AMEN.

Thursday, October 11 (on wising up)

Okay, now (hopefully without sounding too codependent) I
must express my concern for Jenny. I've called her mom
twice this week to see if I might possibly visit Jenny. All I
want to do is to give her a big hug and encourage her. Is
there anything wrong or codependent with that? I think
it's just being a good friend. But the problem is, according
to Mrs. Lambert, Jenny isn't allowed visitors. And for some
reason (maybe it's the way she says things) I'm not totally
convinced that Mrs. Lambert is telling the whole truth. I
may just try calling West Haven for myself. In the meantime, I will keep praying (as will Beanie and Steph).

Now (speaking of Steph) here's the best news I've
heard in ages. Beanie says she thinks it's just a matter
of time before Pastor Tony pops the big question. Of
course, she told me not to say a word about this to Steph
(or anyone), but she says they see each other almost
daily, talk on the phone each night before bed, and she
thinks it all seems pretty imminent. I sure hope so. I think
they make a terrific pair. And I know Tony has been so
lonely after losing Clay last spring. And Steph has
changed so much in the last year. A miracle really. I just
really believe it's meant to be. And I'm so happy for her

(even if it is a little premature to celebrate). Hopefully that's not codependent.

It's really getting so I question myself almost constantly. Although I did get some encouragement from Jesus' words about "loving your neighbor as you love yourself." I got to thinking, now that's <u>not</u> codependent. Maybe that's the reason He said it like that. Because the way I figure it, if you take really good care of yourself and your relationship with God (that's loving yourself), then you won't turn into a codependent when you try to love and help others in the same way. And hopefully they'll appreciate your help. So in a way, it's just really simple. And for that reason, I have decided to stop freaking about this whole codependent thing but to just pray about it instead.

But first one more interesting note. You see, one of my favorite classical authors is Jane Austen and one of my favorite books is <u>Emma</u> (which was also made into a contemporary movie called <u>Clueless</u>, but that's another story). But anyway, I'm thinking that Emma was probably just codependent too. Although I think she got wise and was beginning to finally escape it in the end. But isn't it interesting how much I loved that book and that character? I told Beanie all about this codependent stuff and she just laughed real hard, but finally agreed that I'd probably hit the nail on the head, and that I was lucky to make this discovery now while I'm still young enough to escape turning into a bitter old woman married to some abusive alcoholic. I think she's right!

DEAR GOD, I KNOW THAT YOU'RE THE ONLY ONE
WHO CAN REALLY LEAD ME AND KEEP ME FROM
MAKING A TOTAL MESS OF MY LIFE (NOT TO MEN-
TION THE LIVES OF THOSE AROUND ME). BECAUSE
WITHOUT YOU, I'D PROBABLY JUST TOTALLY MESS
UP BIG TIME. SO PLEASE HELP ME TO BE WISE AND
DISCERNING WHEN IT COMES TO STUFF LIKE
CODEPENDENCY. I REALLY WANT TO HELP OTHERS,
BUT WHAT I THINK I NEED TO DO IS TO ALLOW YOU
TO HELP OTHERS THROUGH ME. PLEASE SHOW ME
HOW TO DO THIS. AMEN.

SIXTEEN

Friday, October 12 (a good day)

At noon, Beanie and I were talking about Jenny (we both miss her and wonder how she's doing), and Beanie said, "Why don't you just call West Haven and ask if she can have visitors or not. And if not, ask why not." So I just marched over to the pay phone, looked up the number, and called. And dontcha know, the receptionist said, "Sure, Jennifer Lambert can have visitors. In fact, we encourage it. Visiting hours are three to five every day."

So it's settled, tomorrow both Beanie and I will visit her. Beanie thought I might like to go alone, but I told her I thought it would be better if she came along too. I think Jenny could use a good support of friends right now, but of course, I haven't mentioned any of this to any of her old friends, who are so wrapped up in their own lives, they don't even seem to notice she's missing. And even if they did know what was up, I'm not sure how much help they'd be. I mean, some of them actually act as if having anorexia were cool. Too weird.

Then an interesting thing happened in my psychology

class today. We were supposed to partner up with someone
for a project, and I was about to ask Anna Parker (a girl
I've known since grade school) but then this guy I barely
know (but seems nice), Trent Ziegler, asked to partner
with me and I said, "Sure, why not." So we went to the
library and started working on this fictional case study
where Trent is supposed to be suffering from depression,
and I'm supposed to be diagnosing him. It's pretty silly, but
our teacher thinks it's worthwhile, and because our
grade is dependent on it, we're cooperating.

So anyway, I say all the normal things to him, but then
I throw in something like, "But have you tried praying?" or
"Maybe you just need to trust God with your life." Well, I
can tell these kinds of comments are really bugging him,
but he's being a good sport and answering the questions
(for his fictional character anyway). But when it was
time to quit, he asked me if I thought those religious
questions were realistic or not.

"I mean, aren't psychologists supposed to be sort of
impartial about religion? Aren't there laws to prevent that
kind of thing?"

To which I laughed and said, "I've never heard of a
law prohibiting any professional from practicing his religion."
Then I thought a moment. "Except, perhaps, in school. But
I've heard of doctors who pray with their patients, and
even attorneys who argue for religious rights. Why can't a
Christian psychologist recommend that his patient pray?"

Trent shrugged. "I don't know. I suppose it couldn't hurt."

"On the contrary, I'm sure it would help."

His brows raised curiously as he held the library door open for me. "I take it that you must be a Christian then?"

I nodded. "That's right. Do you still want to be my partner?" See, this project is supposed to go on for two whole weeks.

He grinned. "Yeah, I suppose it could get pretty interesting."

"Well, I'll try not to come on too strong. But I'll do what I think a good Christian psychologist might do."

"And I'll try to react like a good atheist suffering from depression might act."

Then I laughed. "No wonder my patient's suffering from depression! I would think anyone who doesn't believe in God would get pretty downhearted. I know I would."

Trent frowned, but said nothing. And suddenly I wondered if he might actually be an atheist himself. I don't think I've ever actually met a practicing atheist (although Jenny tries to act like it sometimes), but I didn't really mean to offend Trent by saying that.

"Don't mind me," I said half apologetically. "I just happen to be sold out on God and couldn't imagine my life without Him."

He sort of smiled then. "Well, then that's cool for you. But it might not be like that for everyone else on the planet."

"Believe me, I know. It's just hard for me not to want to share something with others that's been so incredibly life changing for me."

"Yeah, it might be cool to hear a little more about it. You sure don't seem to lack for enthusiasm when it comes to your beliefs."

By then we'd reached the locker bay and it was time to part ways, but I felt like I still needed to say something. "Well, feel free to ask me anything you like about my relationship with God. I'm pretty much an open book when it comes to my faith." I laughed. "Or anything else, for that matter."

"Well, after I'm finished playing the depressed atheist patient, maybe you can play the repressed Christian patient."

I smiled. "Yes, because as you can clearly see, I must certainly be pretty repressed."

"Yeah, but the surface can be deceiving sometimes."

I nodded, not quite sure of how to respond and needing to head to work, I just told him good-bye and hurried on my way. But as I drove to work, I prayed for Trent. Because despite his atheist talk, I suspect he's really searching.

Saturday, October 13 (visiting Jenny)

Beanie and I walked into West Haven at exactly three o'clock. It felt pretty weird too. I mean, I've seen movies with mental hospitals and they all sort of seem alike, and I always figure they just do that for the movies. But West Haven seemed eerily like some of those. It has locking gates and a security check-in, and then you wait in this cold, sterile sort of waiting room, and you hear some pretty strange sounds coming through the reception area (like occasional screams, laughing, and stuff), and it's all a little unnerving. I was so glad that Beanie came with me because she kept making jokes about the whole thing, saying that I better be careful in case they found out about my latest psychological self-diagnosis (the codependent thing) because they just might lock me up too. Which is totally ridiculous because it's not even that kind of disorder. But at least it got us laughing.

Finally, someone came to take us to where Jenny was sitting in a day room. She had her back to us and was looking out a window to where it was raining cats and dogs outside. I was relieved to see she had on real clothes. (I'd been worried she'd be wearing a hospital gown and paper slippers.) But she looked fairly normal in her jeans and sweatshirt.

"Hi, Jenny," I call out, to give her some warning. Then she slowly turns around, but her face (or maybe it is her expression) just doesn't even look like her. Instead of her usual perky smile, she seems sort of flat and blank and empty.

But then she smiles (only slightly) and waves and says hello. And Beanie and I make a big deal of greeting her, then pull a couple chairs over to where she's sitting.

"How're you doing?" I ask, trying not to show how nervous I feel.

"Okay, I guess."

Big, long pause.

"So how's the food?" asks Beanie brightly (and I want to sock her).

Jenny makes a wry smile. "Yummy. That is, if you like

eating through a feeding tube." Then she scowls.

"Ugh, they make you eat through a tube?" I ask, then immediately wonder if that's the wrong approach.

She nods. "Yeah, unless I can start doing it myself."

"Can't you?" I ask hopefully.

Sadly, she shakes her head.

"Isn't there anything you feel like eating?" asks Beanie. "I mean, how about ice cream?"

Jenny makes a face.

"Well, how are you feeling then?" I ask. "Are you feeling a little stronger now that you've got something nutritious in you?"

She just shrugs. And that's pretty much how the next hour goes. And let me tell you, it's not easy. It's one of the longest, most difficult hours I've ever spent, and even though I feel guilty for leaving before visiting time is over, I'm certain that I'll never last another hour, and am pretty sure Beanie feels the same.

"Well, we should be going," I finally say. "I hope we didn't wear you out."

She just shrugs again, for what seems like the hundredth time. But then she says, "Will you come back?"

"Of course," I say, too quickly. "If you want us to, that is."

Then she nods and I notice just the tiniest spark of life in her eyes. "Yes, please do come back."

So we both hug her, and I can feel the tears building in my eyes, but I don't want her to see; I don't want to discourage her any more. So, I tell her we'll be praying for her, and that we'll be back to visit her soon. And as we reach the door, I turn around to see her looking at us with big tears running down her face, but she's not making a sound. Part of me wants to run back and stay, but another part says it's time to go. And when we finally get back out to the parking lot, I'm just feeling totally confused about everything.

"Man, that place is lame," says Beanie. "Poor Jenny."

"Did you see her face as we were leaving?" I ask, barely able to talk.

Beanie nods. "Yeah. But I didn't know what to do. It seemed better to just go. But I think we should go back. Maybe even tomorrow."

"Tomorrow?" I stare at her curiously. But of course, she's made of much stronger stuff than I am. "You want to go tomorrow?"

"Don't you?"

"I suppose so. It's just that right now I'm feeling pretty drained."

"Then you better let God fill you up again."

I sigh. "Yeah, I suppose you're right."

We hardly spoke on the ride home. But Beanie stayed at my house and ate dinner with us, and afterward we went up to my room and rehashed the whole thing. Then Beanie suggested we should pray for Jenny. So we did. And then I felt a lot better. I just hope Jenny does too. I really, really hope our prayers are making a difference because, to tell the truth, it sure didn't seem like our visit helped all that much.

Sunday, October 14 (whose life is this anyway?)

After church, my dad took us to dinner at a Chinese restaurant. And we got to talking about this being my last year at home and how I'd be going to college and everything next year, and then I mentioned that I'd been wondering how important it was for me to go to college. Big mistake.

"You mean, you'd actually consider not going to college?" asks my dad, his forehead creased with fatherly concern.

"Maybe," I say as I use my chopsticks to pick up a sweet-and-sour sparerib. "You know college isn't for everyone."

"But it's certainly for you," says my mom eagerly. "You're an honor student, Caitlin. Why in the world would you choose not to go to college? It sounds absurd."

"Maybe she wants to be a receptionist forever," offers Ben. Thanks a lot, little brother.

"That's not it," I quickly say. "I've just been thinking of other options." Well, to tell the truth, I've only been playing with this idea recently, and I must admit now, it was incredibly stupid of me to voice these thoughts aloud to my family over dinner.

"What options?" demands my dad, at the same time trying to appear calm.

"Well, for one thing, I'm thinking what if I'm not totally sure what I'm going to college for?"

"But your writing," suggests my mom. "You could go into

journalism or English literature or..."

"Or how about psychology?" adds my dad triumphantly. "You were just saying last week how much you like your psychology class."

"Just because I like a class doesn't mean I want to make it my life's profession."

"Well, that's okay," says Mom. "You don't have to decide right away. You can just take general requirements the first year, and then decide later on down the line. I know people who changed their minds clear up into their senior year or ended up with a double major. It all works out."

"I know." I start clicking my chopsticks together in frustration, wondering why it is that parents feel they must control so many elements of your life. I mean, look at Jenny's parents (or more particularly her mom), and where's that gotten her? "Maybe I'd like to just spend a year or two down in the mission in Mexico," I say quietly. "Maybe I could just work to feed and help the children at the garbage dump."

Well, now you should see my parents' faces. It's as if I'd said I thought I might start shooting up heroin or become a surrogate mother or sell off my body parts or something. I mean, they're like totally appalled. Of course, they both say they think it's wonderful how much I care about those little kids, but wouldn't it be so much better if I get my degree first, then go help them later? To which I somewhat testily answer, "You know, it's a funny thing. But when you're a little kid and you're picking through the trash heap for scraps of rotten food, you might just find it a little hard to understand why it takes someone FOUR years before they come down and bring you something to eat!"

Well, naturally that irritates them. And I'm getting more than a little upset myself. So since I've already stuck my foot in it, I just continue. "Whose life is this anyway?" I blurt out. "I mean, who gets to decide what I do or don't do next year? What if God is calling me to be a missionary? And what if He wants me to go to Mexico to feed His starving little children?"

Now my dad kind of rolls his eyes (which really irks me) then says, "Oh, great, so now you want to become Mother Teresa?"

"And what's so wrong with that?" I challenge, locking eyes with him.

"Nothing, honey," soothes Mom, trying to cool things down before we're all yelling and screaming. "But can't you see why we'd like you to finish college first?"

Well, by then my stomach's so knotted that I know I cannot possibly eat another bite. And although I feel just a teeny bit guilty for ruining everyone's meal, at the same time, I refuse to take all the blame for this stupid scene (see, I'm moving beyond codependency!). I stand up and tell them not to worry, but I'll find my own way home, thank you very much!

Then in a calm but firm voice, I say, "This is my life, and I intend to live it however I feel is right. So you better get used to it." Now I'm thinking perhaps that last line was uncalled for. But, sheesh, isn't it the truth? Then I walk out of the restaurant and down the street to a bus stop, where fortunately (since it's starting to get cold and I didn't wear a very warm jacket) a bus pulls up. And as I ride toward home, I question myself, wondering if I am totally wrong to take such a strong stand against my parents. I mean, they are _my_ parents. And we are supposed to respect our parents. But what do you do if you believe God is pulling you one way and your parents are pulling you the other?

About that time, I remember the Bible verse where Jesus said that families would become divided over Him (father against son, mother against daughter). And while it's a little reassuring, I still hope that's not what all this is about. After all, my parents are Christians too. I just don't get why they don't understand this or support me in it.

When I got home, I immediately called up Pastor Tony, hoping I could talk to him and get some answers, but unfortunately he wasn't home, and I really didn't want to leave a message, so I just hung up. Then not wanting to be there when my parents got home, I hopped in my car and took off over to Steph's to pick up Beanie since we'd planned to go visit Jenny today anyway.

Apparently, Steph and Oliver were spending the day with Pastor Tony (the reason he wasn't home). So I sat on the couch and told Beanie all about the confrontation with my parents and how angry and disappointed I was in them. And for the first time since I can ever remember, Beanie sided with my parents—against me!

"Cate, if I had parents like yours, I'd listen to them. I mean, just look at them, they're both well educated and responsible and respectable citizens. And if that's not enough, they're even Christians who go to church. And just for the record, I think they're absolutely right about the college thing. You're way too young to think you can go off and be some missionary in Mexico. You need to finish your education first, and who knows, by then you might even want to do something else anyway."

Well, I felt like I'd just been run over by a Mac truck. I mean, I was totally speechless. But not Beanie. No way. She just kept going. "And besides, Cate, aren't children supposed to obey their parents? And to respect them too? And I don't mean to offend you, but aren't you just a little bit concerned that this whole Mexico missionary thing might simply be your codependent side raising its head again?"

"I—I don't know," I finally said, fighting to hold back the tears. Her words really cut deeply, but my pride kept me from wanting to admit this hurt. "But the thing is," I try, sounding weak. "I don't think anyone should tell anyone else how to live her life. I think it's a private thing between her and God."

"Well, if that's true, then why do you even have friends or parents or pastors? Why do we bother to talk about things?"

"I don't know." I stood up, trying not to show how upset I felt, but failing miserably. "And right now I'm wondering why I even bothered to talk to <u>anyone</u> about this." I walked over to the door. "And you can be sure, I won't again!"

"Oh, don't get mad, Caitlin," she started. "I'm sorry—"

But it was too late. I was outta there.

I drove around all afternoon. And now I'm kicking myself because I never did go in to see Jenny. But I will tomorrow, somehow, even if I have to get off work to do it. I didn't get back home until after dark, and then I went straight to my room. Oddly enough, no one even bothered me. I suppose they think if they leave me alone, I'll cool off and come to my senses and forget all about this Mexico nonsense.

DEAR GOD, I'VE PROBABLY MESSED THINGS UP A LOT BY OPENING MY BIG, STUPID MOUTH TODAY. BUT I REALLY WOULD LIKE TO GO DOWN TO MEXICO TO FEED THOSE KIDS. IS THERE ANYTHING WRONG WITH THAT? I MEAN, I'VE BEEN THINKING THAT IF YOU'RE CALLING ME TO BE A MISSIONARY, WHAT'S WRONG WITH MEXICO? DEAR GOD, ARE YOU SERIOUSLY CALLING ME TO BE A MISSIONARY? OR HAVE I JUST IMAGINED THE WHOLE THING? BECAUSE IF YOU ARE CALLING ME, I'M WILLING. I JUST NEED YOU TO SHOW ME WHAT YOU WANT ME TO DO. AND I SUPPOSE I SHOULD GO DOWN AND APOLOGIZE TO MY PARENTS FOR BEING DISRESPECTFUL TODAY. BUT ON THE OTHER HAND, I TRULY BELIEVE YOU WANT ME TO STAND ON MY OWN TWO FEET AND TO FOLLOW YOUR WILL FOR MY LIFE, EVEN IF NO

ONE ELSE CAN UNDERSTAND IT. BUT I JUST NEED
FOR YOU TO MAKE IT CLEAR WHAT YOUR WILL IS.
PLEASE HELP ME TO UNDERSTAND. AMEN.

Anyway, I did go downstairs and apologize to my parents. I didn't say much except that I didn't mean to be so disrespectful. They were very sweet about the whole thing, and they even apologized too. Thankfully we didn't talk about it anymore. But I did assure them that I was praying for God to lead me. And when I knew where He was leading, I would let them know, and hopefully they'd be supportive. In the meantime, I am keeping my mouth shut tight. I suppose I should call Beanie and apologize to her too, but it's pretty late now, and I hate to wake up little Oliver. I'll just talk to her tomorrow.

SEVENTEEN

Monday, October 15 (amazing stuff!)

Beanie seemed to be sulking today. I told her
I was sorry about walking out on her like that, but that
she'd hurt my feelings. And although she did apologize, it
seemed sort of halfhearted like she didn't really care,
which I must admit hurt my feelings all over again. I
mean, she's the one who said most of that stuff in the
first place. How could she have expected me to just
stand there and take being mercilessly railed on by my
"best friend"? I mean, aren't best friends supposed to side
with you and <u>not</u> your parents? Like, what's up with that?

Well, trying to forget about this thing with Beanie, I
went to work as usual after school, but when I got there I
explained to Rita about Jenny (making her promise confidentiality—not that she knows the Lamberts or anything). I told her how I'd missed visiting Jenny yesterday
and how it would mean a lot to go see her today, and
Rita said, "No problem; you go ahead and you can take
the whole afternoon if you like, it's been dead around
here all day anyway."

So I drove over to West Haven by myself, wondering what I was getting myself into. I mean, it had been tough enough going with Beanie (and she really was a big help). What would it be like to visit there all on my own? But I decided to just pray about the whole thing as I drove along, and during that time it felt as if I put it all in God's hands. A huge relief.

And as a result of putting it in God's hands, you won't believe what happened next!

I'd barely sat down when Jenny asked me where Beanie was. Well, I apologized for that, saying how I'm sure Beanie would've liked to come, but how it was probably my fault for getting into a little squabble with her yesterday.

"What did you guys fight about?" she asked with a lot more interest than she'd shown during our last visit.

Relieved that she was at least trying to support her end of the conversation today, I decided to just go ahead and tell her the whole moronic story. I thought if nothing else, it might help kill time or even make her laugh. And to tell the truth, I wanted something to distract me from this strange girl who was sitting across from us. She just kept staring at me, then making all these odd twisty faces and weird sounds. All of which didn't seem to faze Jenny in the least. I guess she's gotten used to the freaky stuff that goes on there. I sure don't know if I ever could.

Finally, I finished the story, not even sure if Jenny would really comprehend or even care. I mean, why should she—she's got enough problems of her own. But when I was done, she nodded just like she'd actually taken it all in and understood perfectly.

"I know <u>exactly</u> how you feel, Cate," she said with sincerity. "It's so frustrating when your parents try to take over your life. I mean, that's just how it is with <u>my</u> parents. It's like, they've decided <u>where</u> I'll go to college, <u>what</u> I'll major in, and now they'd even like to tell me what and when to eat, not to mention who I should hang with, and how I should talk and dress. Sheesh, I wouldn't even be surprised if they've already gotten me secretly engaged to one of their friends' sons by now."

I had to laugh at that. "So you know what I'm talking about then."

"Yeah, it's like your parents think just because they brought you into this world that they own you body and soul. Like, you should've seen my mom wigging out last summer when I told her I wasn't going out for cheerleading this year. I mean, she acted as if I'd announced that I was dropping out of school or something. And the truth is, I was just sick to death of all that stuff. I mean, I've done it for years now. And I just wanted to be my <u>own</u> self for a change—not my mommy's pretty little puppet girl. But do you think <u>she</u> understands any of that, even now with me sick like this?" Jenny pushed a dark strand of hair from her misty eyes and looked around the stark day room. "I mean, <u>even in here</u>, she still wants to control me."

"Do you think that has anything to do with why you quit eating?"

She looked down at her hands in her lap. "Well, that's what my shrink suggested."

I reached over and touched her shoulder. "But you know your parents <u>don't</u> own you, Jenny. Don't you?"

"Sometimes I think I do. Other times, I'm not so sure. I mean, think about it. They're the ones who pay for everything. They put a roof over my head, buy my clothes. And they'll pay my college tuition. Right now they pay for my care here, which, my dad keeps <u>lovingly</u> reminding me, is <u>not</u> covered by insurance and is <u>not</u> cheap."

I glanced around nervously, thinking perhaps she didn't really need this kind of stressful conversation that I'd brought on. But then again, maybe she did. "But if you had to, Jenny, I'm sure you could support yourself without your parents. Not that you'd ever need to do that."

She shook her head. "I'm not so sure."

"I bet you could, Jenny."

"Yeah, maybe." Then she studied me curiously. "Caitlin, do you really, truly think you could just pack it all up and take off for Mexico to feed those garbage dump kids like you said? I mean, not just talking, but for real."

I carefully considered her question, then tried to answer as honestly as I knew. "I think if that's what God was calling me to do, then with God's help I could probably do it."

"Even if your parents totally disowned you?"

"Well, I don't think they—"

"But what if they did?"

"Then I'd just have to follow my heart and simply do

what I believed God was telling me to do."

"But how would you get by? I mean, where would you get money to live and stuff?"

"I'd just have to trust God for everything I needed. I'd have to trust Him to take care of me as well as provide what I needed to give to the kids. I know it probably sounds crazy—"

"No, not totally."

I smiled. "Actually, I think it would be kind of exciting. That is, if I was absolutely certain it was God's will for me to do it. And I think it'd be fun."

"Yeah, it sounds kind of fun to me too."

"Really?" I stared at Jenny in disbelief. Was she pulling my leg?

"Yeah, I really do. And I can guess what you're thinking right now. You're probably wondering how a girl who cannot even feed herself might ever imagine that she could go down there and help feed all those starving Mexican children. Right?"

I shrugged. "Yeah, sort of."

"Well, I've been actually thinking about those starving kids the last couple days and thinking how they'd probably give anything for all the food I've just thrown away during the last six months or so. And let me tell you, that makes me feel totally rotten."

"That's not good."

"Yeah, but more than that, it makes me feel really furious too. Not just angry with myself, but at my parents as well. I mean, I realize this whole thing isn't totally their fault. I'm the one who originally quit eating. But according to my shrink, and I'm starting to believe him too, a large part of this is the result of how they've treated me."

I nodded. "From what I've read, I think you're probably right about that."

"And yet, I know that I'm the only one who can fix this mess I've gotten into. It's pretty much up to me right now."

"Yeah, Jenny, but I really believe that God can help you too."

"Well, it might surprise you to know that I've actually been thinking about God lately."

"Really?"

She nodded firmly. "And I told myself yesterday, if you and Beanie came back here again, I was going to ask you both to pray for me. Right here. Just like the time you prayed for me at my house. Remember?"

"Yeah."

"So would you?"

"Pray? Of course. I've been praying for you a lot."

"I can tell."

So then I just sat there and bowed my head and prayed for her. Even with that girl making all her weird noises in the background. I prayed for several minutes, and just before I finished, I even prayed for that girl. And then I waited quietly for a few moments, just in case Jenny wanted to actually pray too. But it didn't seem like she did, so I just said "Amen," and then looked up to see her crying once again.

But this time, it didn't seem like that same kind of crying as before. For some reason I felt there was a little bit of hope mixed in with her tears. Then I reached over and hugged her for a long moment. And I could tell she really appreciated it.

"You know what I did just before you said amen?" she asked as she wiped her nose with a Kleenex.

I shook my head, still feeling somewhat amazed about what had just happened.

"Well, I didn't actually say the words out loud, but silently, and in my heart, I asked God to just take over my life and do something with it."

"Oh, Jenny, that's so great!" Now I started crying too and hugged her all over again. "And He will, Jen. I promise you, if you let God, He really will!"

"I believe that now."

"I'm so happy for you!" Then I noticed the girl across the room. To my surprise, she was just sitting quietly now, still watching us, but she seemed more peaceful somehow.

"And do you know what?" Jenny laughed a little. "My parents will probably really freak over this because they've always said that religion is a crutch for weak people. And they'll probably be all ashamed of me for giving in to it like this. But you know what? I don't even care what they think. And, to tell you the truth, I can't wait to tell them I'm a Christian now." Then she frowned a little. "I am, aren't I? I mean, I didn't say the words out loud or anything, but won't it work just the same?"

Then I quickly explained what I've heard Pastor Tony

say so many times about how being a Christian simply means that you've invited Jesus Christ, God's Son, into your heart. "When I did it, I was all alone in my room and I can't even remember exactly what I said, but I think I wrote it all down in my diary. But basically I just gave my heart to God."

She nodded vigorously. "Yes, that's exactly what I meant when I prayed that. I hope that's enough."

I laughed. "Don't worry, Jen, that's enough. Now, you just need to keep praying and allowing God to lead you. And I'll bet He'll even help you to be able to eat food and get well."

She smiled what seemed a real and honest smile (and it was so good to see it). "I think He can help me through this, Catie. Somehow I really do."

Well, by then it was already a little after five o'clock and I wondered how two hours could pass so quickly. But I explained to her that I'd try to visit again this week, but that it might be tricky since visiting hours conflicted with my work schedule. She said it was all right and that she understood. Then I promised to come both days during the weekend and to call her if I couldn't come by during the week.

"And maybe you and Beanie can patch it up," she suggested. "Because I'd really like to see her again too."

So, let me tell you, I was flying higher than an overfilled hot air balloon as I drove home from West Haven. I was thinking, Hey, I _am_ a missionary, after all! I mean, it's just like Pastor Tony said. God _can_ use me to reach out to the people He's placed all around me. And, believe me, I give all the credit for what happened today with Jenny to God! And I think it's just totally cool!

EIGHTEEN

Friday, October 19 (busy week)

What a totally fantastic week this has been! I got to go visit Jenny again yesterday (for just an hour) and it was absolutely great! She seems like her old self—only better! She's started eating again and she says it's because God is healing her. And she told me how this really nice nurse who works there (and who just happens to be a Christian) gave Jenny a New Testament Bible to read. And she's been reading it all week, which she says is making her mom pretty furious, although I suspect Mrs. Lambert tries to hide it. But Jenny says it makes no difference to her because this is her life. To which I say, <u>Go girl!</u> I'm so proud of her.

Well, Beanie and I did sort of patch things up, but she still didn't go with me to see Jenny yesterday although she did promise she'd go tomorrow. We'll see. I'm not sure what's up with her, but something seems to be bugging her. Maybe tomorrow we can talk it out.

Something else has been going on this week too. Trent, my partner in the psychology project, has become very interested in hearing about God. It seems like it's all we talk about. And he even wants to get together with me this weekend to talk some more. Okay, now I'll admit this concerned me a little at first, because I'm thinking, is he really interested in God, or is he interested in me? Now I'm not trying to be all narcissistic or anything, but I realize that I do need to watch out for these kinds of things. Anyway, I explained to him today that I'd be happy to talk to him more, and I even invited him to church, but I made it clear that I don't date. This seemed to really amuse and intrigue him, and he wants to hear more about that too. So, we're going to meet at the library tomorrow night (we also need to do some additional research for the project), and I'll try to answer all his questions as best I can.

But to be totally honest about this whole thing, I must say that Trent is a very nice looking guy (in that Tom Cruise sort of way), and not only that, but he seems really sensitive and kind and caring. And also intelligent. He's enjoying our psychology class so much he's considering majoring in it in college. And all this to say that, yes, if I were a girl who wanted to date, this is just the sort of guy I might go for (that is, if I weren't a Christian because he is definitely NOT). I suppose this troubles me a little. I mean, it would feel lots better and safer if I were meeting a geekish sort of guy at the library tomorrow. And it's not that I think Trent would necessarily try to pull anything, but maybe more that I just don't totally trust myself yet. But then I'm thinking that's pretty ridiculous. Besides, we're just meeting to talk and to study. That's all! So I guess I'm just being overly paranoid about the whole thing. Maybe it has to do with the role I've been playing in our psychology project. I'm now role playing that I'm the paranoid Christian girl who thinks everyone is out to get her. Pretty funny, really. <u>As long as it just doesn't actually rub off on me!</u>

Saturday, October 20 (what a day!)

Sheesh, so much has happened today that I'm not even sure if I can get it all down. But I guess I'll just start at the beginning and work my way through.

Well, the day started out pretty weird (I mean after I did my Saturday chores and stuff). I went over to get Beanie to go have some lunch (and hopefully talk). And when I got there she was all by herself and crying. So I drove her over to the Bagel Shop and bought her lunch, and then gently asked her what was up.

"I'm not supposed to say anything," she said as she sipped hot chocolate and looked like she'd lost her best friend. Which I felt pretty sure she hadn't since I was sitting right across from her.

"What do you mean you're not supposed to say anything?" I demanded with mild irritation. "I'm your best friend. We're not supposed to keep secrets from each other."

"I know. But I promised."

"Beanie, I guess I shouldn't push you to tell me something. I mean, if you really don't want to. But you're clearly miserable about something, and as your best friend, I only want to help."

She looked right at me and I could see her eyes filling with tears again. "Well, maybe you can guess what it is. That wouldn't exactly be telling you."

"Okay," I began, ready for the game. "Let's see, it's a secret. Does it have to do with Zach?"

She shook her head, then brightened a little. "But I did get a letter from him this week."

"Good. Okay then, is it your mom?"

"Well, not exactly, but it might involve her."

Hmm, now she had me wondering, but I still felt stumped. "Beanie, can't you give me some sort of clue or anything?"

"Well, it's something I should be happy about."

I studied her for a moment, then it came to me. "It's about Steph, isn't it?"

She kind of shrugged, but I could tell I'd hit pay dirt.

"Steph and Tony are engaged, aren't they?"

"You didn't hear it from me." Then she looked at me with pleading eyes. "Please, don't tell anyone. Not your mom or anyone. They're going to make an official announcement in church tomorrow so everyone will hear it at the same time."

I smiled. "That's so great! But now, why are you so upset about it? Don't tell me you've developed some kind of schoolgirl crush on Tony and you're getting all jealous now?"

She sort of laughed. "Yeah, you bet. No, it's just that

I'd hoped I could live with Steph until graduation."

I nodded. "Okay, I get it now. So you're getting all worried that you'll have to move back home."

"Yeah. Please don't breathe a word of this, but they plan to get married fairly soon, maybe even during Thanksgiving weekend."

"Oh." I thought a moment. "But Beanie, you know you could come live with us."

She looked at me skeptically. "Thanks, Cate, but you know your parents don't really like me all that much."

"That's not true," I argued. "I mean, there was a time when they weren't that crazy over you, but that's all changed."

She rolled her eyes. "Yeah, like when? Maybe it was when I got pregnant. I'm sure I really impressed them then. Or maybe it was when I got so depressed—"

"Beanie, my parents have changed lately."

She kind of laughed. "Yeah, like when you were telling me they were trying to run your life last week."

"But you sided with <u>them</u>," I said accusingly, still feeling the sting of her choosing them over me.

"Not really. I was just pretty upset because Steph had told me about the whole engagement thing. And I suppose I was feeling jealous that you have decent parents who actually care enough about you to try to tell you how to live." She sighed deeply. "Now that's a problem I wouldn't mind having."

Suddenly I felt just totally horrible for having been upset with her on Sunday. "I'm so sorry, Beanie. I wish I'd known all this then. I can see how tough this must be for you."

"I just don't want to move back with my mom."

"Beanie, I'm serious, you can move in with us. I'll gladly share my room with you and everything."

"I appreciate it, but it's not really your decision, Caitlin, now is it? And I hate putting that kind of pressure on your parents. I've sensed their disapproval in the past. I'd just hate it if they played the 'good Christians' and let me come live there but were unhappy about it underneath. You know what I mean?"

"Yes. But I think I could talk to them honestly and figure this all out first. And I wouldn't encourage you to live with us if I felt they really didn't want it." Then another possibility occurred to me. "You know, Beanie, I've been saving a lot of money from my job. I wonder if we both worked, if we might possibly be able to afford a place of our own."

She laughed. "Do you know how much even a cheap apartment costs? And then we'd have utilities and food, and I just couldn't ask you to do that, Caitlin. I mean, you're set just fine. I'm the one who needs a place."

"And you wouldn't consider staying with Steph and Tony? I'm sure they'd welcome—"

She held up her hands. "Steph already said as much. But I said forget it. I refuse to live with newlyweds. I told Steph I'd still come baby-sit for her so she and Tony could enjoy going out and stuff, but I will NOT live with them."

"Yeah, I can kind of understand. But please, at least

let me talk to my parents. You might be surprised at how they really think of you."

"Sure, go ahead and ask. I'm sure not in any hurry to ask my mom. She's got a new boyfriend who's living at her house right now. I've seen his motorcycle parked there at all times of the day, which makes me suspect that he doesn't even have a job."

"Poor Lynn. She really ought to improve her taste in men."

Beanie laughed sarcastically. "Or just give them up altogether."

After lunch we walked around the mall for a while and picked out a book to take to Jenny, then we headed over to West Haven. But when we got there, her mom and dad were in there talking to her, and the nurse said we'd have to wait. So we waited and waited and even considered leaving, but then I thought if her parents were making it hard on her, she might appreciate seeing us, even if only for a few minutes before visiting hours ended. Then just before five, her mom and dad left without even acknowledging us, and then we were allowed into the day room.

Jenny seemed slightly upset, but she smiled to see us coming toward her. And we both hugged her and gave her the book.

"Thanks so much for coming," she said. "I suppose you saw my parents leaving just now." She shook her head then sat down. "Now I sure could've gotten by without that little visit."

"Jenny," exclaimed Beanie cheerfully. "You look so good! Are you feeling better now?"

Jenny nodded. "Yes, I've actually been able to eat, not to mention keep down real food this week. My shrink is so pleased with me."

"Caitlin told me that you've become a Christian," said Beanie quietly. "I think that's so cool."

"Yeah, me too. Unfortunately, my mom thinks I'm totally losing it."

"But isn't she glad you're eating again and getting better?" I asked. "I would think she'd be so relieved that she'd be glad you've a Christian."

Jenny laughed, but her eyes looked sad. "Well, you'd think so. But according to my shrink, my mom is a real control freak, and anything I do outside of her wishes will probably upset her."

"What did your shrink think about you becoming a Christian?" I asked with real curiosity (thinking about the project I'm doing with Trent).

"He's not a Christian himself, but he thought it was great because it was helping me to get better."

"Good for him."

We talked until about five-fifteen, and then a nurse came and told us it was time to leave. We hugged Jenny again and told her we'd try to return tomorrow for a longer visit. Then I asked if I could bring her anything.

"Remember that chocolate cheesecake?" she said as the nurse was shooing us toward the door.

I laughed. "You bet! I'll bring enough for all of us." I

glanced over to where that same strange girl was sitting, then added, "and then some."

"Thanks," she called as the door shut behind us, the lock bolting into place.

Beanie seemed in much better spirits after that, and I even told her about my plans to meet Trent in the library this evening. She gave me a curious glance, then said, "I've seen him around school. He's not too difficult to look at, if you ask me."

"Want to come join us?" I offered, unsure of whether I wanted her there or not, and just thinking that thought troubled me a little.

"Yeah, it'd be fun, but I promised Steph I'd watch Oliver tonight. The two lovebirds are going out to celebrate their secret engagement."

"Well, they might as well enjoy their secrecy now because it sounds like it'll be all over with by tomorrow."

So now I'll get to the part of my day that's a little confusing, to me anyway. I met with Trent as planned. We worked on our project for a little while, but the main librarian kept telling us to "Shhh!" so finally we just left and headed over to Starbucks where we could make as much noise as we liked. We ended up just talking. And I must admit it was fun. I refuse to lie about it—something about being in a coffee shop and talking to a good-looking guy is an altogether enjoyable experience. Yet at the same time, I feel guilty for enjoying myself. Like, did I think I was out on a date? No, not really. We drove separate cars, I bought my own café mocha, and we <u>never</u>

touched. So, is that a date? I don't think so. But I'm not totally sure. And the reason I'm not sure is because I really like Trent. I like talking with him. I like his laugh. I like looking at him. And that's what got me worried.

And I can tell he likes being with me. In fact, when it was all said and done, he says, "Too bad you don't like to date, Caitlin."

To which I say, "It has nothing to do with liking to date. I just choose not to date because I believe that's what God has shown me is best for me." Now, I'd already explained this whole thing to him once before, and he seemed to understand, but I think what he meant now was that he wanted to ask me out. So I think I made myself perfectly clear.

Then we just said good-bye and parted ways, and that's when I started to actually question my commitment to God about not dating, thinking how an innocent evening like this couldn't really hurt anything. And, let me tell you, that really bugs me a lot! I'm thinking, there I go and make this big promise to God just a few months ago, and then some good-looking guy comes along, and BAM, I start second-guessing myself and my commitment. Sheesh, how shallow is that?

So when I got home, I came up here and turned back in my diary and carefully read what I actually wrote about dating and boys and sex and everything. A good reminder! And what I believe God showed me then is still completely right for now. And so I think I'm back on track. But it really troubles me to see how easily I might get derailed. I know I'm human, but I thought I was stronger than this. And, sheesh, Trent isn't even a Christian! Although I do believe he's searching. For sure, I plan on praying for him and continuing to share my faith. And I'm thinking if Jenny Lambert can get saved, well then so can Trent Ziegler! In fact, I may just ask Jenny tomorrow if I can tell him about her.

DEAR GOD, PLEASE FORGIVE ME FOR QUESTIONING A VOW I MADE TO YOU. I KNOW YOU HAVE SHOWN ME THAT DATING, FOR ME, IS A PROBLEM. I ADMIT I AM WEAK IN THIS AREA. BUT THE BIBLE SAYS THAT YOU CAN BE STRONG IN MY WEAKNESS, AND SO I GIVE MY WEAKNESS TO YOU. I ASK THAT YOU WILL USE ME TO SHOW TRENT WHAT YOU'RE REALLY ABOUT, IN THE SAME WAY THAT I BELIEVE YOU USED ME TO REACH OUT TO JENNY. I THANK YOU FOR WHAT I LEARNED TONIGHT. I THANK YOU THAT YOU ARE WORTH FAR MORE TO ME THAN A DOZEN TRENTS OR JOSHS OR EVEN CLAYS (AND YOU KNOW HOW SPECIAL CLAY IS!). SO PLEASE DON'T EVER GIVE UP ON ME, GOD. I MAY BE STUPID SOMETIMES, BUT I'M REALLY TRYING. AMEN!

NINETEEN

Sunday, October 21 (busy day)

Pastor Tony invited Steph up to
the pulpit today, then he made his "little" announcement
and the whole church just clapped and cheered. And I
will never forget the look on Aunt Steph's face. I'm sure
I've never seen her look so completely and blissfully happy.
And when I think of all she's been through in the past several years, I am so amazed at how much God has done in
her life. It's miraculous really. I'm just so totally glad for
her, and I must admit, a little proud too (nieces can be
proud of aunts!).

Mom was so jazzed that she threw a small impromptu
engagement party for them, just family and close
friends, but it was fun. And as I was helping her get
things set up beforehand, I mentioned how upset Beanie
was to think she'd be going back to live with Lynn. And
Mom said that was too bad, but at least Beanie would
graduate next spring and then be able to move on. Well, I
wanted to bring up the subject of Beanie living here, but
the timing seemed a little off, and remembering what

happened at the Chinese restaurant (another case of bad timing, I think), I decided to just cool my jets and wait a while.

Besides, Beanie had seemed to be in pretty good spirits today when we went to visit Jenny. Thankfully, this time Jenny's parents weren't there. In fact, they never even came at all today. Jenny said they're like that. "They just come when they want to and never tell me exactly when to expect them or not to. Sometimes I feel like I'm just a great, big inconvenience to them, not to mention an embarrassment of late."

Well, I for one was relieved not to have them around. And with Beanie making a little drum roll on the table, I opened the pink bakery box containing a whole chocolate cheesecake and Jenny actually licked her lips.

"Okay, I've been a really good girl," she said cheerfully. "And I'm eating their food, which is no small feat considering how it tastes like mushy cardboard and is generally pretty darn disgusting. So believe me when I say this looks fabulous, dawling."

Beanie located a helpful nurse's aid who quickly rounded up some paper plates and forks (and was rewarded with a piece of cheesecake). Then I looked over to where that strange girl was sitting once again (and I'm thinking she's probably about our age, maybe older; it's hard to tell since she acts sort of childish). But anyway, I asked her if she'd like a piece. She nodded shyly and came over to the table.

"Hi, Rachel," said Jenny in a friendly voice. "These

are my friends, Caitlin and Beanie." Rachel just nodded, took her cheesecake with both hands, then returned to her exact same spot on the couch to eat it.

"It must be hard being here," said Beanie as she took her piece.

"Yeah," said Jenny. "I mean, at first it was totally horrible, nightmarish even. I even felt like I must be crazy too. I figured that most everyone in here was. But lately I've gotten to know a few of them, and they're really not all that bad. Sure, like me, they have their problems and phobias and stuff, but they're really not totally nuts, not all of them anyway. In fact, in a weird way, it's kind of interesting being here now."

"Yeah, well, it's not your everyday experience," I said, taking a bite.

"And I've taken your advice, Caitlin, and I've started journaling. My shrink thinks it's great therapy, and I guess it kind of helps me to see everything in a different light."

"Yeah," I agreed. "My diary came in handy last night when I started second-guessing myself about my nondating rule."

"See!" said Beanie, pointing at me triumphantly. "I told you meeting Trent last night would be pushing it."

"Trent?" asked Jenny with a suspicious raised brow.

Then I explained to her about our psychology project and how we'd nearly gotten ourselves thrown out of the library, and then talking at Starbucks until late and everything.

"I had Trent in my biology class last year, and I must

admit he caught my eye too. But since he wasn't exactly involved with my group—" she made a fake gagging sound—"well, I just never looked at him too seriously. Pretty dumb, huh?"

"I guess." I set down my fork. "But he's a really nice guy, and I honestly think he's searching for God in his own way although he does call himself an atheist."

Jenny laughed. "You've got to watch out for those ones who call themselves atheists." She pointed to herself. "They're usually the ones who are searching the hardest."

"Yeah." I laughed. "I remember when Josh told me that you were an atheist last year. I'd almost forgotten about that."

"Well, that's what I liked to claim. But I think what I was really doing was just begging someone to step up and prove me wrong. I think I wanted to believe in God but just couldn't. So I made this big deal of calling myself an atheist, just hoping someone would set me straight."

"That's interesting," said Beanie. "You know, my mom makes a big deal about not believing in God too. She always made fun of me for going to church and stuff. And she really loved arguing with me about religion. It used to drive me nuts."

"Sounds familiar," said Jenny as she licked the last creamy bite from her fork. "Thanks, Cate, that cheesecake was superb."

We stayed there until five again, just talking and joking. Then I asked Jenny how much longer she'd need to be in here.

"Good question." She rolled her eyes. "On one hand, I think I'm well enough to go home, but on the other hand, the idea of living at home with my mom constantly on my case is kind of scary." Her voice grew quiet. "I mean, what if I start doing it again?"

"But aren't you all better now?" asked Beanie.

"My shrink says some people never get completely over this. And even if I get released, I'll still need to go to weekly counseling and then into some sort of support group."

"So do you think he'll be releasing you soon?"

"I think so." Then her eyes grew sad. "And it's not like I really love it here or anything, but in a way it does feel safe and secure. I'm just afraid I might not be ready to go home yet."

"Wouldn't it be cool," said Beanie suddenly, "if we could all three get a place of our own to share."

"Yeah, sure," said Jenny sarcastically. "Like maybe we should all go out and start buying lottery tickets or something."

"Yeah, it's just a stupid idea." Beanie looked slightly chastised.

"No, not really," said Jenny quickly. "I'm sorry, Beanie; I didn't mean to sound so cynical. I just wish it were really possible."

We hugged her and told her good-bye, and then I dropped Beanie at Steph's and headed straight home where I'd promised to help my mom before the party. And now that it's time to go to bed, something has occurred to me about all this. It might be totally ridiculous, but who knows?

> DEAR GOD, I'M FEELING A LITTLE CONCERNED (AND HOPEFULLY NOT CODEPENDENT) ABOUT BEANIE AND JENNY TONIGHT. PLEASE TAKE CARE OF BOTH OF THEM. GIVE THEM A GOOD, SAFE PLACE TO LIVE WHERE THEY CAN FOLLOW YOU AND TRUST YOU FOR ALL THEIR NEEDS. AND THANK YOU FOR BRINGING TONY AND STEPH TOGETHER. I'M SO GLAD FOR THEM AND HAPPY THAT LITTLE OLIVER IS GETTING A REALLY GREAT DAD. THANK YOU SO MUCH! AMEN.

Thursday, October 25 (Grandma comes through)

Well, I've been working all week (or maybe it's God who was doing the working) on that idea I got on Sunday. Anyway, when we had our little engagement party, my grandma was feeling bad because she's already made her usual plans to go to Arizona and flies out on the first week of November to stay until March, and now she's all worried that she'll miss the wedding as a result.

But anyway, she was also boo-hooing that the lady who usually house-sits for her (keeping her plants and her ancient and beloved cat, Marigold, alive) just bailed on her saying she can't do it this year. So anyway, I've been talking to Grandma this week about the possibility of Beanie house-sitting for her (thinking that perhaps Jenny could join her too, if need be). And Grandma happens to really like Beanie (she always has), and she's noticed how Beanie's just wonderful with Oliver (not to mention saving his life!), and she also thinks she was a real godsend to Steph. So anyway, she said she'd give this idea some serious consideration, and that she'd talk to Steph and see what she thought about the whole thing. And tonight, Grandma called me up and said she thinks it's a great idea, and she was, like, so glad I thought of it!

Afterwards I tried to call Steph's to talk to Beanie, but the line was busy (probably the lovebirds saying good night). But I'm thinking Steph might've already told Beanie anyway. And now I'm just so happy and relieved that she has a place to live, besides with Lynn.

Of course, I don't know that this will make any difference for Jenny (who goes home with her parents on Saturday), and I didn't even mention this other situation to Grandma yet, although I bet she'd be open to the idea. She's a pretty kind and understanding person. In fact, I'm wondering why I haven't been more involved with her lately. Because for an older lady, I think she's pretty cool!

T W E N T Y

Friday, October 26 (hard work)

Tonight our youth group spent the
whole evening (until after midnight) working on stuff for
the Harvest Party that our church plans to give next
week. It's like an alternative to Halloween for the kids, so
they can come and do carnival games and stuff. We'll
be working on it all weekend, but it's really pretty fun.
And it's great having the whole youth group working
together on something again. But now I'm so exhausted I
don't think I can write another word.

Saturday, October 27 (atheist meets youth group)

Today, Trent called me up and asked if I had time to
get together and talk with him tonight. And I told him I
was working on the Harvest Party preparations, but if he
wanted to come along and help, I'd be happy to talk with
him. And since he sounded sort of down or depressed, I
hated to just say no, forget it. But to my complete surprise, he agreed, and he turned out to be quite helpful in
getting the Go Fish booth set up, then afterwards a

bunch of us sat around and drank Dr. Pepper and talked
until pretty late. Trent asked a lot of good (and hard)
questions about God, and everyone was really honest
and helpful. Trent seemed relieved that we didn't try to
have an answer for every question or to explain everything to him. I mean, like who really knows how many animals were on Noah's ark or if the sand was wet where
the Red Sea divided!?! And several times we just had to
say that our belief in God is based on faith and trusting
in things we can't always see. But that we know in our
hearts that it's real and true and we wouldn't give it up
for anything. And although Trent didn't like fall on his
knees and get saved, he did thank us for talking to him.
And now I'm pretty sure the whole youth group will be
praying for him. Takes a load off me!

    I had invited Jenny to join us tonight, but her mom
said no. Big surprise there. But now I'm wondering if Mrs.
Lambert plans on locking Jenny up until she graduates.
And if she does, how long will it take until Jenny quits eating again? Oh man, would I like to give that woman a
piece of my mind! What's up with parents these days anyway? I mean, Beanie's mom doesn't care at all. Jenny's
mom seems to care way too much. Sheesh, my parents
are looking better and better all the time. Although I still
haven't raised the issue of what I think about becoming
a missionary with them again.

    To be honest I'm almost afraid to consider the whole
thing too much. But I have gotten some interesting books
about missionaries (including the Jim Elliot one and one

that his widow wrote too; now talk about an amazing woman—she stayed down there with their baby and continued to work with the very same Indians that killed him!). Anyway, my interest in this whole thing is not going away. If anything, I think it's growing. And so I keep praying that God will lead me and direct me. I mean, I realize that college is important. But I also realize that those kids (at the dump) have very immediate needs. And it's some consolation to me when I send money every couple of weeks (by the way, I came up with the acronym: FAD for Food At the Dump, kind of silly, but it works). Anyway, there's still a strong desire inside me to actually go down to Mexico and live right there by the dump and to really roll up my sleeves and help care for those kids myself. And I think, what's wrong with that? But then I really do know what could be wrong (besides my concerns about codependency). I could be just doing what I want and not what _God_ wants. And I realize how that could just totally blow up in my face. And so all I want is that God would show me what I need to do. In the meantime, I'll do everything I can think of to raise money for FAD.

Wednesday, October 31 (boo!)

Our Harvest Party was a _screaming_ success tonight. And Jenny's mom surprised us all by letting Jenny out of her cage (as Jenny calls it) and allowing her to come help out at the party. I'm not sure if her mom knew it was a church-related thing or not since we held it at the VFW lodge. I think Jenny just told her it was for a good cause. Which, as it turns out, it was!

My best surprise of the night was when the party was all over and we were cleaning up (man, what a mess!), and Pastor Tony walks in and announces that most of the proceeds will be donated to my Mexican FAD fund. Well, talk about happy! I couldn't believe it. Then even though I was tired, I worked extra hard.

But another nice surprise was that Trent came tonight and actually helped out at the Go Fish booth. And he seemed to be having a really good time with the kids too. And I noticed he and Jenny sort of hit it off, which I must admit gave me some mixed feelings. Okay, I know I'm not interested in dating or having a boyfriend, but I admit that I've enjoyed his attention. Is that so wrong? Maybe. I'm not totally sure. But when I saw him joking with Jenny, I think I got just a teeny bit jealous. But I never showed it. And I quickly got over it. And now I kind of hope that they become friends. Who knows, maybe God will use Jenny to reach Trent! On the other hand, I just hope Trent doesn't pull Jenny down. Although she seems like she's getting stronger and stronger in her faith these days. It's weird how that works sometimes. It almost seems the harder a person's life is, the harder they hold on to God. Makes me think we all need to have a really hard life or something. Although I'm sure that's not really true. I guess we just need to realize how lost we all are without God, and then to appreciate how great it is to have Him! Even tonight, when I felt just a little "off" because of the thing between Jenny and Trent. But because I turned to God and shared those feelings, I suddenly felt so much better. And happy too.

Saturday, November 3 (fun day)

Last week, Tony and Steph invited Beanie and me to go out for dinner with them. And then, just as we sat down, Steph said she couldn't wait any longer and asked if we would consider being her bridesmaids. Well, we were both so surprised and honored—and of course we said yes! And today, we three went shopping for dresses.

Fortunately (since there's not much time), Steph and Tony want to keep it simple and inexpensive so we only looked at dresses we could buy right off the rack. And wonder of wonders (I'm sure God had a hand in this), we found them all in one shop! Steph's dress is a tea-length gown of creamy white lace (it looks like something from the Victorian era), and Beanie and I will both wear tea-length satin dresses made of this luscious, coppery color that's sort of iridescent. Absolutely gorgeous (even if it isn't my best color). Steph wants everything to be in fall colors (golds, rusts, olives), and she plans on having chrysanthemums everywhere (she says they're cheap but pretty).

Now, since our church meets in the school, this presented a small problem for the wedding location, but my mom suggested that Steph check into having the wedding at our old church (which has brick walls and stained glass and looks all very proper and churchlike), and both Tony and Steph agreed to this. Tony has a pastor friend coming from New York to officiate, and it just seems like everything is falling right into place. As my grandma says (and she just left for Arizona today) "that's what happens when you live right." Well, I'm not totally sure about that because I know there are lots of people who try to follow God and live right, yet have all sorts of trials and tribulations coming at them (you should read some of these missionary books I've got!). But I am totally glad for Steph's sake that it's going pretty smoothly (she's gone through enough hard stuff in her life) and it's good to see things falling into place for her now. She's a little sad to see Beanie moving out to my grandma's, but Steph understands. And it didn't hurt when Beanie and I offered to keep Oliver over there during the honeymoon after the wedding.

So next weekend we'll look for shoes to go with our dresses. In the meantime, Beanie and I are planning a big wedding shower for Steph (we read in Bride magazine that the bridesmaids are supposed to do this), and we really don't have all that much time to get it together. We'll just invite friends from church and family and stuff, and Beanie wants to host the whole thing at Grandma's (which she already got permission to do). She will officially move in tomorrow. I'm going to help her, not that she has all that much to move, but it'll be fun seeing her get set up. I asked if she felt scared or nervous about living in a house all by herself and she just laughed, then reminded me of some of the things that used to happen when she lived with Lynn. Yeah, living alone sounds a lot safer!

Sunday, November 4 (moving day)

After church, Beanie and I loaded my car with everything she had at Steph's and took it over to Grandma's house. It was kind of weird watching Beanie pull out the key and unlock the door as if she lived there (which she does!), but I suppose I'll get used to it. Then Beanie asked if we could swing by Lynn's place to get some of the things that Beanie had never moved (since Steph's apartment was pretty crowded) so we drove over to Lynn's.

"I sure hope we don't see that Harley parked in the yard," said Beanie. "I'm not really looking forward to meeting this loser."

I was actually hoping that no one would be home. I never enjoyed seeing Lynn, and I know how hard it could be on Beanie. But when I pulled up we saw Lynn's old beater car sitting in the driveway. "No motorcycle," I said, trying to sound positive. "Do you want me to come in and help?"

"Do you mind?"

"No." Not really a lie. I mean, I didn't mind helping Beanie although I did mind having to talk to Lynn.

Beanie knocked on the door and we waited for a pretty long time. Then finally Lynn opened the door and we both just stood there and stared. Lynn, still in her bathrobe, had a swollen and cut lip, a badly bruised cheek, and a black eye.

"What happened to you?" asked Beanie in a flat voice.

"What do you want?" snarled Lynn.

"I came to get my stuff," said Beanie, folding her arms across her front.

"What stuff?"

"My things," said Beanie, growing impatient. "Things I left in my room."

Lynn stood there, her eyes narrowed, just staring at the two of us. Then she stepped aside, letting the door swing open and said, "Well, come on in, girls. As you can see, I cleaned especially for you."

Well, the place looked just as bad (maybe worse) as the last time we'd been there (when we'd cleaned and made our quick getaway over the back fence), only now the air was especially stale from having been closed up due to the cooler weather and the whole place reeked of cigarette smoke. I silently followed Beanie to her room where she told me what to take. I could tell this was stressing her out and tried to be as helpful and support-ive as possible. It took quite a few trips since she didn't have any boxes to put things in.

On my last trip through the house, I noticed Lynn sit-ting on the sofa with her head hanging down and looking about as dejected as I've ever seen anyone look. And suddenly, I'm not sure what happened, but it seemed like I saw her in a whole new and different light. Maybe it was God giving me a glimpse of the way He sees her. But suddenly I was looking at her, and she just seemed like a broken little girl. A poor, abused little girl, who was lost and confused and desperately needed someone to love her. Well now, it's no secret that I've never had a good relationship with that woman, but right then and there, I silently prayed that if I was supposed to say something that I'd know what it was, and that I'd be able to say it. So I paused for a moment, then said, "Lynn, it looks like life has been treating you kind of rough lately."

She looked up at me and sort of squinted like she wasn't even sure who I was or why I was standing in her living room, then she said, "When hasn't life treated me rough?"

I nodded, trying very hard to remember that little girl and to show sincere empathy. "I know; it must be pretty hard."

She ran her hand over her bruised cheek. "Yeah, I don't know why I don't just give up."

I looked at a dingy chair across from her. "Can I sit down?"

"Sure." She rolled her eyes with sarcasm. "Make yourself at home."

I sat down and looked evenly across at her. "Did your boyfriend do that to you?"

"Ex-boyfriend."

"Well, that's probably for the best."

She lit a cigarette. "Yeah, I suppose if I had any sense, I'd just swear off men altogether."

I nodded. "Yeah, that's pretty much what I've done."

She looked at me curiously, then took a long drag

from her cigarette. "You telling me you've sworn off men, Caitlin?" She laughed.

I chuckled too. "Yeah, something like that."

"What's the deal? You turn into a lesbian or something?"

"No." I laughed loudly now. "But God showed me it wasn't in my best interest to date guys. It just seemed to lead me into places where I don't really need to go."

Now she looked clearly confused. "God showed you what?"

"That I needed to give up dating."

"You gotta be kidding."

I shook my head and now noticed that Beanie was standing like a shadow in the doorway to her bedroom. So I continued. "I know it sounds kind of crazy, but I can't tell you what a huge relief it is not to worry about all that dating stuff anymore. Now I can just focus on what's really important."

She exhaled a long stream of blue smoke. "Like what?"

"Like my life and school and friends and God."

"God again." She ground out the cigarette in an overly full ashtray.

"Yeah, without God, I'm pretty sure my life would be nothing but a great, big, fat mess."

"You mean like mine?"

"I wasn't saying that."

"Yeah, but that's what you mean, isn't it? You think my life is just one big, stinkin' mess, don't you? Go ahead,

Caitlin, admit it!" She stood up now, her voice growing loud. "I know you're always looking down on me—you and those picture-perfect, little yuppie parents of yours, just like June and Ward Cleaver. I know you guys all think I'm nothing but poor white trash. Don't you?"

I stood too, unsure of what she might do in her anger. "No, Lynn." I spoke calmly, hoping to soothe her ruffled feathers. "I don't think that at all." I paused to take in her messed-up face, realizing how underneath that she was actually still quite pretty. And then I suddenly felt tears filling my eyes. "To be honest, Lynn, I might have thought like that before—before I started seeing things differently. But now, I just think you've had a really rough life, and it's taken its toll on you. And it just makes me incredibly sad. Sad for you. And sad for Beanie too."

She exhaled loudly, almost as if my words had somehow deflated her, and then she sank back down onto the couch. "Yeah, well, it makes me pretty sad too."

I paused for a long moment, then sat back down, silently begging God to give me the exact words that Lynn needed to hear. "You know, it doesn't have to continue like this."

She just shook her head. "Nothing ever changes for me. I just get older and uglier and pick out worse men is all. But no matter what I do, nothing ever gets any better."

"It could get better, Mom," said Beanie, clearing her throat as she stepped into the room.

"I knew you were there listening," said Lynn matter-of-factly, without even looking up.

"Mom, I love you," said Beanie, her voice breaking. "And I really want to see things get better for you. Do you know that?"

Lynn nodded, swallowing hard. "I know, baby. I know."

"But you're the only one who can make things change," said Beanie.

"I know, but I can't."

"You can!" demanded Beanie. "But only if you let God help you."

Lynn looked up, her eyes now filled with tears. "Look at me, Beanie, and tell me honestly. Do you really think— if there even is a God—that He would give a flying fig about someone as messed up as I am?"

"First of all, I <u>know</u> there is a God," said Beanie. "And second of all, He loves everyone no matter how messed up we are."

Then I jumped in. "And sometimes it's only when we realize how messed up we are that we can understand how much we need to call out to God for help."

"And what if I did that?" She looked intently to Beanie, then back to me. "What if I did call out for God to help? And what if He just wasn't there? Or didn't answer? What then?"

"He is there," said Beanie quietly. "He will answer."

"And you'll never know if you don't ask," I added even more quietly, worried that we were both pushing Lynn too far and too fast, and that any moment she might just blow up on both of us.

She sat there for a long time, just gently rubbing her

arm, which I suspect was also hurting from the beating her Harley man had given her. And the whole time, I just kept praying. Praying that she wouldn't blow up, praying that she would listen, and praying that for once in her life she would just call out to God.

Finally she stood. "Well, I'm sure you girls need to be on your way."

"But, Mom—"

"Just go!" cried Lynn, swinging her arm as if to defend herself. "Leave me alone! Just get out of here, both of you! Leave!"

Beanie nodded to me, and we both moved toward the door; then Beanie said, "I'm praying for you, Mom."

"Me too," I added as we stepped out to the porch. Then we heard something crash against the wall and break into pieces.

"It's okay," said Beanie. "Probably just an ashtray, her favorite form of projectile."

I looked at Beanie. "Are you okay?"

She smiled. "Yeah. That was great."

"Great?"

"Yeah, I've never seen her listen to stuff about God that well before."

I kind of laughed, then we got in the car and drove over to Grandma's where we hauled all Beanie's stuff into the laundry room.

"This is so totally cool to have a washer and dryer right in the house," said Beanie with unashamed appreciation.

I nodded, thinking how little I knew of real suffering.

TWENTY-ONE

Thursday, November 15 (catch up time)

The past two weeks have been so wild and busy that it's almost a blur in my memory. And consequently I've neglected my diary. I'll try to catch up if I can, although it won't be easy.

The first thing I want to share is that I'm going to go to a missions conference! Now I'm sure that sounds pretty boring to the average person on the street, but I am just totally jazzed about it. Our youth pastor, Greg, was planning on going, and last week he told our youth group all about it. It's this really big event where thousands of kids who are interested in missions come from all across the country to attend. It's called Urbana (and is somewhere near Chicago). It happens right after Christmas and lasts until New Year's. Anyway, Greg invited anyone interested to come along. He's going to drive a church van.

So far a quiet guy named Rick from McFadden and I are the only takers, but I am so excited I can hardly wait. At first my parents were all, like, no way, that's too far away, you need to be home during Christmas vacation, and on and on. So I just quietly told them (no ranting, no raving) why I wanted to go, and that I'd pray that God would speak to them, and then I left it at that. Well, it took about a week, but finally they told me they'd talked about it and decided I could go. Of course, they've not paying for it, which is fine (I have money in savings), but I'm just glad that they willingly agreed. I had really prayed that God would soften their hearts. And let me tell you, I really did not want to have a great big fight. So I was hugely relieved. Of course, they had to tack on a little parental lecture about how this didn't mean they thought it was okay for me to skip out on college and hop down to Mexico to live at the garbage dump. I bit my tongue, then told them I understood their concern. But the whole time, I'm thinking, we'll see about that! Anyway, I'm just glad I get to go to Urbana.

Okay, now I'll tell you about Jenny. She had her eighteenth birthday on November 10 and moved out of her parents' home on November 11. First, let me say I don't think that moving away from your parents while you've still in high school is such a great idea, but in Jenny's case I totally agree. Plus, she'd met with Pastor Tony several times for counseling help, since she was starting to turn all anorexic again as a result of all the stress and pressure her mom was dishing out to her. And Pastor Tony actually called my grandma who's soon to become his mother-in-law to make sure it would be okay for Jenny to stay there with Beanie. And of course, Grandma was totally cool about the whole thing and even said she was glad for Beanie's sake and that she didn't really like the idea of a young girl being there all on her own. So now Beanie and Jenny are roomies and both living in Grandma's house. Beanie stays in my mom's old bedroom, and Jenny has Aunt Steph's. Now isn't that just too funny?

But in order to cinch the deal, Pastor Tony had them both sign a contract with my grandma (his idea not hers) saying they won't have boys over, drink alcohol, or smoke, or anything else that my grandma wouldn't approve of. And they both signed with absolutely no argument. And within days, Jenny seemed to get better—she's eating again and even cooking too! She says she just really needs to feel like she has some control over her own life. She was a little worried at first because she had to leave her car at home, and she was afraid her parents wouldn't pay for her college, not to mention how she'd manage to afford food. But she and Beanie both got jobs at Pizza Hut. Okay, so it's not the best place in the world, but the bus goes straight there, and they get all the pizza they can eat. But then after that, Jenny's dad started to secretly send her money. Pretty nice, I think. So Jenny's sitting pretty right now. And I expect she's helping Beanie out too.

Jenny said that Trent asked her out, and she told him she didn't want to date right now! Well, that kind of surprised me. I mean, it's not like I'm trying to get every-one to follow my lead and give up dating (not that that's such a bad idea). But I asked her what was up with that, and she said she just felt like she needed time on her own (without a guy) to get healthy. Then she told me a bunch of stuff about Josh (and what went on with those two last year), and it almost made me want to quit writing to him forever and just punch him in the nose the next time I see him. But now I realize that's wrong (it's not like I wasn't aware of a lot of that stuff), so I just need to forgive him all over again. But just the same, it still irks me.

What is it with guys anyway? Okay, I know they're not all just looking for a "good time," and I know Josh has changed (at least, I HOPE he has), but I still sometimes think it's a dangerous dating world out there for teens. And I literally thank God for sparing me from it.

The good thing about Jenny turning Trent down is that we can all hang together as just friends now. And I think Trent actually likes that. I guess he's never really had a real girlfriend before. And he just has brothers, so this is the first chance he's had to get to know a girl— and most of the time he has three of us (Jenny, Beanie, and me) so he's pretty glad about that. As far as his atheist thing, he's still holding out. But we act like we don't care, and like we think it's just a matter of time until he comes around. It's become a bit of a joke with us. But I think he appreciates that we don't pressure him too much but just love him for who he is. And isn't that what Jesus would do anyway?

Well, I know I've probably missed a few things, but it's

late and we have a full day of cleaning, cooking, and decorating tomorrow (getting everything ready for Aunt Steph's bridal shower) so I'm going to hit the hay.

Saturday, November 17 (shower surprises)

Well, we slaved all day until Grandma's house was totally spotless. I think even she would be impressed. We polished the silver and got out the good china (I called first to see if it was okay). My mom bought flowers (all in fall colors to go with the other decorations). And Jenny had this crazy idea of making these little cakes called petit fours that her mom makes sometimes, so she actually called her mom for the recipe, which she thinks impressed her mom (no small feat), and we spent most of the day mixing, baking, and decorating these teeny, tiny little cakes. But let me tell you, it was worth it! Everyone just loved them.

But okay, let's back up the truck now and start at the beginning of the shower. You see, it was supposed to start at seven-thirty, but at seven o'clock, someone knocks on the door (we're still frantically trying to clean up our last mess in the kitchen), so I run out hoping it's not some church lady showing up early (I mean, we haven't even had a chance to change out of our dirty clothes yet) and I open the door to see Grandma standing there with a big, beautifully wrapped box in her hands!

"Grandma!" I screamed, throwing my arms around her. "We didn't expect to see you until next week for the wedding."

She handed me the box and laughed. "Well, I had no problem exchanging my ticket since Thanksgiving weekend is always so booked. And I thought I sure don't want to miss that shower. I would've let myself in, but my hands were full and I wanted to surprise you."

So the next thing, we had Grandma helping to clean in her own kitchen; the whole while she just oooed and ahhed over everything. It made us feel so good. Then we ran upstairs to change. And I went into Beanie's room.

"Uh, Cate," she said a little uncertainly. "I need to tell you something."

"What?" I asked as I pulled a sweaterdress over my head.

"Well, at the time, it seemed a good idea, but now I'm getting a little worried."

"What?" I asked again, getting impatient since it was almost seven-thirty.

Then I realized she looked like she was about to start crying. "I'm so stupid! So stupid!"

I grabbed her by the arm. "Beanie? What is going on?"

"I invited my mom to the shower!"

Well, that room was so silent we could hear my grandma happily humming downstairs. And I felt as if someone had just dumped a bucket of ice water over my head. I just stared at her in horror, hoping that I'd heard her wrong. "You what?"

She nodded. "I know. It was incredibly dumb. Totally stupid. Moronic even. What was I thinking?"

I'm thinking, What were you thinking? But instead I

say, "Why did you invite her?"

She had tears in her eyes now. "Well, she called last week, and she sounded so sweet and sad on the phone—totally unlike her usual self—and she said how she hadn't been with a guy since that Harley dude and how she had also quit drinking and was thinking about going to AA."

"Oh, Beanie, that's great."

She nodded and swallowed. "And I told her so too, and she asked what I was up to, and I mentioned the wedding and shower. And then I just couldn't help myself; I invited her to the shower." Followed by a big sob.

I nodded slowly, trying very hard not to say what I thought. I mean, Lynn Jacobs (barfly, wild woman, Harley chick) at a wedding shower with a bunch of church ladies, and poor Aunt Steph who's about to become a pastor's wife. Well, it was all just too much. I sank down onto the bed and sighed. "Do you think she'll really come?"

"All week long, I've been telling myself, no way, she would never come. I mean, she knows what your family all think of her. And she knows Steph, and they've even exchanged words—like when I moved out and then at the hospital." Beanie started to cry. "Oh, I'm so sorry, Caitlin."

"Beanie, it's okay." Now I took in a deep breath, trying to calm myself. "I mean, if she's really on the bandwagon and doing good, what are the chances of her really showing up? I mean, she'd realize that wasn't a good thing."

Beanie perked up. "You're absolutely right! She would

know better than to come here." Then her face fell. "But on the other hand, if she's been drinking or—oh no!"

I looked at my watch, just minutes before seven-thirty, then I grabbed her shaking hands. "Beanie, let's pray!"

So we stood there and prayed the fastest prayer ever, that God would watch over everything tonight and make it a good and memorable time for Aunt Steph.

"That's all we can do," I said with confidence I wasn't fully assured of. "Now, it's time to face the music."

And already they were starting to arrive. Jenny was in charge of taking coats, Beanie took gifts, and I offered them coffee or tea, the whole while thinking at any given moment this whole thing could fall totally apart or explode in our faces.

"Caitlin," whispered my mom as I handed her a cup of tea. "You girls have done a beautiful job putting this together."

I smiled and said, "Let's just hope it stays together." And that's when I noticed Jenny open the door to see Lynn Jacobs standing on the porch. Without saying a word, I headed straight to the door, determined to do whatever was necessary to preserve peace.

"Hi, Lynn," I said, forcing a big smile to cover my terror. Then I noticed she had a nicely wrapped gift in her hands, and she actually looked pretty good. Okay, maybe not quite like a church lady, but she wasn't wearing a plastic miniskirt and six-inch-high platform shoes either. "Come on in. Have you met Jenny yet? She's

Beanie's roommate." Jenny took Lynn's furry coat with wide eyes. (She's already heard a whole bunch of wild Lynn stories.)

Then Beanie stepped up, and I tried to convey to her through a glance that it was so far so good. "Hi, Mom," said Beanie, her voice coming out in a squeak as she reached to take the gift. "I'll put that with the others."

"Can I get you some coffee or tea or punch?" I asked, the same silly smile still frozen on my face.

"Sure, coffee, black. Thanks."

With shaking hands I poured her coffee, my ears straining to hear the background chatter behind me, fearing that any moment it could all blow sky-high and we'd be reading about it in next week's church bulletin. As I quickly returned to Lynn with the coffee, I saw Steph getting up and making her way over. "Lynn," she exclaimed, sounding sincerely glad. "It's so good to see you. I'm so glad you came." Then she reached out and actually hugged her.

Lynn smiled. "Congratulations, Steph. I hear you landed a really good guy."

Steph beamed. "Yes, I can't wait for you to meet him. You are coming to the wedding, aren't you?"

There was an uncomfortable pause, but Steph jumped right back in. "You know, everything's been such a crazy rush. I mean, you'd think it was a shotgun wedding or something." She laughed and Lynn seemed to relax a little. "But since Beanie's one of my bridesmaids, I just figured for sure she had invited you. You will come, won't you? Have you seen Beanie's dress yet?"

"I haven't, but I'd like to."

"Oh, Beanie," said Steph. "Take your mom upstairs and show her the dress. I'll bet she'll love it too."

Well, after that, everything just went as smooth as the buttercream icing on our little petit four cakes. And, not for the first time, I found myself thinking how Aunt Steph is really and truly cut out for this pastor's wife stuff. I mean, I have never seen anyone so genuinely kind and gracious in my whole life. Pastor Tony is one lucky (or should I say blessed) fellow!

AND SO, DEAR GOD, BEFORE I TURN IN FOR THE NIGHT, I MUST SAY THANK YOU, THANK YOU, THANK YOU. I BELIEVE YOU REALLY RESCUED US TONIGHT. AND I BELIEVE YOU ARE DOING SOMETHING REALLY MIRACULOUS AND AMAZING IN LYNN JACOBS'S LIFE. I PRAY THAT YOU WILL CONTINUE TO LOVINGLY DRAW HER TO YOURSELF. AMEN.

TWENTY-TWO

Sunday, November 25 (a quiet moment, at last)

Wow, and I thought the week before last was busy! Well, let me tell you, this last week has been nothing but one big whirlwind. First, we had Thanksgiving at our house—with Beanie and LYNN (no kidding and she was fine) and Jenny and Grandma and Tony and Steph and Oliver, which made for a very full table. But it was great and we all played charades afterwards.

Then later that evening (and to my surprise), Josh and Zach stopped by. They're both home from college this weekend. It was so fun to see them, and Beanie and I thought that they'd both grown up a lot. It was a little uncomfortable at first, what with Jenny there—I know how she and Josh never really did patch things up very well from last year. But by the end of the evening, all five of us were just laughing and joking and having a really fun time. And I must admit, I liked seeing Josh, and I think he liked seeing me. Just the same, my no dating rule stands, and he knows it. But he said he had something he wanted to tell me privately. I said maybe after the wedding since I knew it would keep me fairly tied up for the following day. And both Josh and Zach said they'd be at the wedding too, so I knew I'd see him again.

We all got up early the next day. We had to go pick things up and get the church decorated and all kinds of last minute stuff. And by the time we needed to dress for the wedding, I felt nearly exhausted. But something happened after I took a shower and put on that gorgeous gown. I was revitalized and ready to make it through what turned out to be a very long evening. But oh, was it beautiful. Fall flowers and glowing candles everywhere. Tony wore a dark brown tux, and Steph looked absolutely gorgeous. The only thing that went wrong was that Oliver ate too many mints and threw up during the reception, but everything else was just beautiful. I'd like to have a wedding just like that someday. That is, if I ever get married.

Well, if Josh Miller's eyes were any indication about whether I will ever marry, I'd say my chances are pretty good. Okay, I'm not exactly setting the date. And I know it's ridiculous to even think of such things. I mean, I am, after all, just seventeen. But a girl can dream, can't she? And since I've given up dating, I think I should still be allowed a few, sweet, innocent dreams. But anyway, Josh came up to me during the reception and just stared. I mean, he ogled.

"You look like a princess, Catie," he said in this quiet, serious voice. And do you know that I never seem to mind

when Josh calls me Catie (or anyone else, for that matter—do you think that's maturity kicking in?).

"Thanks," I said happily, then tried to change the subject. "Wasn't that a great wedding ceremony?"

He nodded. "But really you look great. I'm thinking it's
a good thing you're sticking to your no dating rule." Then
he frowned. "You are, aren't you?"

"Sure. Nothing's changed."

He seemed to sigh in relief. "Well, that's good."

Now that confused me a little. "I know it's good. But
why do you say that, especially when you used to question the whole thing?"

He smiled. "It just means no other guy is going to come
along and steal your heart."

Well, I had to laugh at that. "Thanks, Josh. I'll take
that as a compliment."

We didn't get to talk too much at the reception
because there were photos and the receiving line, and I
felt kind of bad because there were a number of times
when Josh was making his way toward me and something
or someone would unwittingly cut him off.

So right after Tony and Steph made their getaway
and Beanie caught the bouquet (which was pretty funny
all things considered), I went and found Josh and told
him I was sorry I'd been so busy that I hadn't been able
to talk to him, and if he had time tomorrow, maybe we
could meet or something.

"Now that wouldn't be a date, would it?" he asked
with a raised brow.

"No. It would be two friends simply getting together to catch up. How about Starbucks tomorrow?"

We agreed on the time, and the next morning I got Beanie to cover for me with Oliver, then went over to meet Josh. And when I saw him, it happened again, that little rush that catches me by surprise and makes me a little uncomfortable. But I ask you, what normal, red-blooded American girl wouldn't feel that way? I mean, he looked so cute and collegiate in his khakis and sweater. Be still, my heart, I jokingly warned myself as I walked toward him.

We ordered our coffees and sat at a tall table. And I could tell something was troubling him. "What's wrong, Josh?"

"It's kind of hard to explain, Catie. I mean, I'm afraid it'll sound kind of lame and dumb. Although I think you might understand."

"I'll sure try." I took a sip of coffee. "Go ahead."

"Well, I suppose it all started on our Mexico trip." He looked up from his coffee. "Hey, how's your fund-raising going?"

I suspected he was avoiding something but went ahead and filled him in on the latest, including the new name, FAD. "It's kind of a silly name, but it's easier than explaining everything all the time. I just hope it doesn't give the impression that I'm not serious about it or that it's just a passing whim or something."

He laughed. "Don't worry. I think we all know you're pretty serious about those kids."

"Okay, enough about that. Tell me what's going on with you. Got a girlfriend who you're madly in love with and getting married next week?"

He rolled his eyes. "Actually, I've been trying to take your advice and avoid that sort of thing altogether."

"Seriously?"

He nodded. "And let me tell you, it's not easy. I mean, some girls can be pretty pushy."

I had to laugh. "Tell me about it. Some guys can be too."

We both shared a couple stories, but then I still felt like he had something that he wasn't telling me. "Josh, it seems like something is troubling you."

"Yeah, back to that. You see, I haven't told anyone about this, and for some strange reason, I think you might understand. But it sounds so stupid to say it out loud."

"Come on, Josh," I urged him. "Think of all the embarrassing things I've told you. We're friends; you know you can trust me. Don't you?"

He nodded. "Okay, like I said, I think it started in Mexico. But I didn't know it at the time." He paused, and I suddenly wondered if this had to do with Andrea and their relationship. Had Josh suddenly discovered that she was the only one for him?

"Go on," I said, growing impatient.

"Well, okay, then I went to college, and I started going to this Bible study and then to a church that these guys go to. I really like this church; it reminds me a lot of Faith Fellowship, only it's even bigger." He paused and took a drink of coffee, obviously still stalling.

"Yeah?"

"Well, one Sunday, not too long ago, this really weird thing happened." He paused again, kind of making a face.

"Yeah?" I'm trying not to strangle him, but I really hate it when people string me along like this.

"Okay, I'll just say it. I think God has called me to be a missionary."

Well, blow me down! I literally almost fell off my bar stool. I mean, I had never written Josh a single word about the whole thing that had happened to me; nothing at all about the missionary stuff. I mean, I didn't even understand it all myself, and I knew I could never explain it in a letter.

"Caitlin?" I heard him saying my name, kind of like if I'd fainted and was flat out on the floor and just coming to. "See, I told you it would sound crazy."

I shook my head, barely able to form words. "Not crazy."

"But I can tell you're shocked. And if you're shocked, I can't wait to hear what my parents will think." He shook his head. "And here's what's really crazy—I actually WANT to do it. Can you believe that? Josh Miller a missionary!"

I nodded. "I can believe it."

"But isn't it weird?"

I nodded again. "Pretty weird." But then I was starting to smile.

"Why are you grinning like that?"

Now I was starting to giggle. "I can't help it."

He frowned slightly. "Are you laughing at me?"

"No." And then I proceeded to tell him the whole story about how I thought God was calling ME to be a missionary too, and how much I'd struggled with it at first, and how my parents had totally wigged out when I said I wanted to go to Mexico next year.

"You mean without even finishing college?"

I nodded. "Yeah, I figure those kids are hungry right now."

He grinned. "Well now, I thought I was a little extreme, but you're something else, Caitlin O'Conner."

Then I told him how I was even signed up to go to a missions conference the very next month.

"Really? Do you think it's too late for me to sign up?" he asked eagerly.

"Check with Greg tomorrow," I suggested.

"I'll call him today."

We talked for about an hour, and it was totally amazing how we had both gone through so many of the exact same emotions and personal turmoil as a result of this strange calling. Then I finally said, "Do you really believe it's God leading you in this direction, Josh?"

"As weird as it may sound, I do."

"Me too."

"Do you think it's just a coincidence that we both have been experiencing the same thing?" I could tell by his expression that his question was utterly sincere.

"I don't know. I've heard Pastor Tony say there's no such thing as coincidences."

He nodded, then cleared his throat as if he had something to say that was going to be difficult. "Do you think this means we'll end up together, Catie?"

Well, I made myself laugh, just to lighten the moment. "I don't know, Josh. But I hope we'll always be friends. It seems God has given us a really special friendship, don't you think?"

"Yeah." He seemed relieved.

"Well, I promised Beanie I'd be back by noon," I said, suddenly uncomfortable.

"Yeah, my folks wanted me to have lunch with them. And I was thinking I'd tell them about this whole thing today."

I felt my brows rise up.

"You think that's a bad idea?"

"No." I paused, remembering the day at the Chinese restaurant. "Just go easy on them, Josh. It's a hard thing for parents to understand and take in all at once. I think they imagine us marching off into deep, dark Africa never to be seen or heard from again. Just go easy."

He smiled. "Thanks for the advice."

Then we hugged, a purely platonic hug (well, that's what I keep telling myself anyway). And now, I'm back at Grandma's, and Beanie and Jenny went out, and Oliver's taking a nap. It's all quiet, and I'm still in a partial state of shock. Josh Miller wants to be a missionary?!?!!!??

TWENTY-THREE

Tuesday, December 25 (happy birthday, Jesus!)

Yes, I know, it's been eons since I've written in my diary. I'm not even sure why. Other than life's been busy; I've been writing to Josh a lot lately, finals at school, work, hanging with Beanie and Jenny, youth group, and stuff. I guess my life is just very, very full. And I know that's all a result of God's hands. For which, I am forever thankful.

Believe it or not, we are on the road right now. I'm sitting in the back of the church van. We had to leave early this morning, but for the most part, our parents seemed to understand (thanks to Tony giving them a little parental pep talk, I think). Josh is sitting up front, right next to Greg, and they've been talking nonstop for hours. Rick (the quiet one) is right behind them, reading his Bible.

Yes, it's kind of weird that I'm the only girl along, but that's okay. We'll drive all day and all night, taking turns sleeping and driving, and we should make it to Urbana by midday tomorrow, in time to register and find our rooms in the college dorms. I have this wonderful sense of excitement, like something really big and powerful is going to happen to me, like God is going to crystallize all these things that have been bouncing around inside of me.

I've studied the brochure carefully and feel like I pretty much know what to expect. There will be speakers and workshops, and then there will be an area set up with booths from all the various mission groups. I'll be looking for a group that knows something about feeding kids on garbage dump heaps. Yes, it sounds kind of silly, but I feel pretty sure they'll be there and that they'll understand exactly what it is I'm talking about. And I'm expecting God to give me some definite direction, like whether to go directly to college or to take a year off to explore some of these things. And I'm willing to do <u>whatever</u> He says. I just need to know what that is. And my key verse for this conference is from Proverbs 3:5-6, and perhaps this will be the key verse for the rest of my life. Not a bad one to have.

It goes like this:

Trust in the LORD with all your heart
and lean not on your own understanding;
in all your ways acknowledge him,
and he will make your paths straight.

And so that's what I'm doing. And it's amazing how peaceful that makes me feel inside. Kind of like nothing can go wrong because I'm holding on to God's hand. Or better yet, He's holding on to mine. And I'm pretty sure if I should accidentally let go, He will still be hanging on. And let me tell you, that really takes the pressure off. Did it concern me that Josh was coming along to the missions conference with us? Okay, to be honest, it bothered me a little bit, just to start with (because I didn't want anything to distract me from what God is showing me).

But then I prayed and got over it, and now I'm totally glad. I mean, it's pretty exciting to have a good friend along who's going through a lot of the same stuff. And I know that we both understand each other and our commitments, and so I'm not worried about anything turning into a "distraction." It's a good feeling to know that we are both growing up these days, not only in ourselves, but in the Lord also. And I cannot wait to see where God is leading us. What a totally wild, fun, and wonderful ride it's going to be!

THANK YOU, GOD!

a personal note from Caitlin...

Dear Friend,

Do you feel like God is nudging at your heart to make a commitment to Him—any sort of commitment? It's best not to put it off, you know. Hey, remember what happened to me???

So,...I invite you to sit down right now before God and consider how He may be leading you. Is He asking you to give Him your heart today? Is He asking you to dedicate your body to Him first and abstain from sex until after marriage? Can you hear His voice speaking to you?

Sometimes it helps to write this kind of promise down. You can do that in your diary like I did, or you can write it down here. Then hide it away if you like, but just don't forget it. Because a promise like this is important—both to you and to God. Because you're His child, and He's always listening.

Blessings!

Caitlin O' Conner

≈ My Promise to God ≈

I, _____ make a vow to God
    Print Name Here

on this day _____ that my heart belongs to Him.
              Print Date Here

And I make a vow to God, with His help, to abstain from sex

until I marry.

_____
Your Signature

THE DIARY OF A TEENAGE GIRL SERIES

ENTER CAITLIN'S WORLD

DIARY OF A TEENAGE GIRL, Caitlin book one

Follow sixteen-year-old Caitlin O'Conner as she makes her way through life—surviving a challenging home life, school pressures, an identity crisis, and the uncertainties of "true love." You'll cry with Caitlin as she experiences heartache, and cheer for her as she encounters a new reality in her life: God. See how rejection by one group can—incredibly—sometimes lead you to discover who you really are.

ISBN 1-57673-735-7

IT'S MY LIFE, Caitlin book two

Caitlin faces new trials as she strives to maintain the recent commitments she's made to God. Torn between new spiritual directions and loyalty to Beanie, her pregnant best friend, Caitlin searches out her personal values on friendship, dating, life goals, and family.

ISBN 1-59052-053-X

WHO I AM, Caitlin book three

As a high school senior, Caitlin's relationship with Josh takes on a serious tone via e-mail—threatening her commitment to "kiss dating goodbye." When Beanie begins dating an African-American, Caitlin's concern over dating seems to be misread as racism. One thing is obvious: God is at work through this dynamic girl in very real but puzzling ways, and a soul-stretching time of racial reconciliation at school and within her church helps her discover God's will as never before.

ISBN 1-59052-890-6

ON MY OWN, Caitlin book four

An avalanche of emotion hits Caitlin as she lands at college and begins to realize she's not in high school anymore. Buried in course-work and far from her best friend, Beanie, Caitlin must cope with her new roommate's bad attitude, manic music, and sleazy social life. Should she have chosen a Bible college like Josh? Maybe...but how to survive the year ahead is the big question right now!

ISBN 1-59052-017-3

THE DIARY OF A TEENAGE GIRL SERIES

ENTER CHLOE'S WORLD

MY NAME IS CHLOE, Chloe book one

Chloe Miller, Josh's younger sister, is a free spirit with dramatic clothes and hair. She struggles with her own identity, classmates, parents, boys, and—whether or not God is for real. But this unconventional high school freshman definitely doesn't hold back when she meets Him in a big, personal way. Chloe expresses God's love and grace through the girl band she forms, Redemption, and continues to show the world she's not willing to conform to anyone else's image of who or what she should be. Except God's, that is.

ISBN 1-59052-018-1

SOLD OUT, Chloe book two

Chloe and her fellow band members must sort out their lives as they become a hit in the local community. And after a talent scout from Nashville discovers the trio, all too soon their explosive musical ministry begins to encounter conflicts with family, so-called friends, and school. Exhilarated yet frustrated, Chloe puts her dream in God's hand and prays for Him to work out the details.

ISBN 1-59052-141-2

ROAD TRIP, Chloe book three

After signing with a major record company, Redemption's dreams are coming true. Chloe, Allie, and Laura begin their concert tour with the good-looking guys in the band Iron Cross. But as soon as the glitz and glamour wear off, the girls find life on the road a little overwhelming. Even rock solid Laura appears to be feeling the stress—and Chloe isn't quite sure how to confront her about the growing signs of drug addiction...

ISBN 1-59052-142-0

Diary of a Teenage Girl, Chloe book 3
Road Trip by Melody Carlson

Monday, August 30

(driving through Wyoming)

It's been almost three weeks on the road now, and I hate to admit it, but some of the glitz has worn a bit thin lately, or maybe it's just getting tarnished. At least for this girl anyway. On the other hand, Allie is still flying higher than a Pop-Tart. Between Allie, Laura, and me, Al's probably the best candidate for a life of fame and fortune. Not that we've seen too much of that since we've only played the state and county fair circuit so far, hanging out with the cows and quilts and raspberry preserves. We've seen more of the Midwest than I ever imagined existed and logged in more miles than I can track. I suggested we get one of those maps with stickers of the states on it, but Allie said that would be lame. I'm not so sure.

We've also hit a few "megachurches" along the way. Last night we performed in a Colorado Springs church with about five thousand people in attendance. Just your average Sunday night service. Talk about overwhelming. I can't imagine ever fitting in at a church that size. Although I'm sure it works for some people, and the pastor seemed like a pretty cool dude. Just the same, it really makes me appreciate my little church back home where I know everybody by name.

Anyway, I think we've done about ten performances so far. Even so, it's safe to say that "Redemption" hasn't exactly become a household word yet—at least not as far as the name of our band goes. Hopefully the word "redemption" is still common in most households.

And backing up here, I don't mean to criticize Allie about her seamless adaptation to our new "celebrity" status. Although sometimes I expect she'd like to do an interview with Robin Leach, telling him about how fantastic it is for a drummer to suddenly be living the lifestyle of the "rich and famous." Ha.

But to be perfectly honest, I think sometimes I almost envy her. Like the way Allie can walk into a room holding her head at this cocky little angle as she coolly scopes out the situation from behind her wire-rimmed purple shades. (I think this is becoming her signature.) And I'm rather impressed with how this sixteen-year-old girl can put out that rock star persona and actually get away with it. Whereas I feel completely stupid and conspicuous whenever I act like that. And believe me, I've tried it a couple of times.

"Just chill," Allie told me yesterday when I was trying to sneak away from an impromptu signing that was making me feel claustrophobic. "This is no biggie."

I rolled my eyes at her, then forced a smile to our gathering of "groupies," who appeared to be in middle school.

"She's just shy," Allie told the girls who were patiently waiting for her signature. "She'll grow out of it someday."

At least this made them laugh. But I still felt dumb. Maybe I'm just incredibly insecure or socially inept. I'm not even sure what exactly it is that impairs me in this particular area. But the sad fact is: I feel unbearably self-conscious sometimes. Now that probably makes absolutely no sense when you consider how I like my appearance to be slightly shocking, or at least that's what some people say. To me, I look perfectly normal. I mean, sure, I've got my piercings, my egg-plant-colored short hair, and what some people consider a weird wardrobe, although it suits me. But those are not the things that make me self-conscious. It's something else entirely. I'm not even sure what, well, other than basic don't-look-at-me-too-close insecurity. Fortunately, I don't feel like that when I'm on stage playing my guitar.

Thank God, I am perfectly comfortable up in the lights when we're performing. It's as if all my fears just melt away. I'm sure I'm more comfortable than Allie up there, since she still suffers an occasional bout of stage fright. Although she hasn't barfed on my guitar recently.

Still, it bugs me that I do come slightly unglued when we're just hanging and people start pointing or staring at us as if we've just been beamed down from a UFO. And I don't particularly like it when they ask for our autographs. But as I've mentioned, Allie thinks it's totally cool. She literally thrives on it. I just don't get it. For the life of me, I don't know how a person can prepare herself for this kind of intense attention.

I mean, talk about weird—having perfect strangers walk up and ask you to sign your name on their programs or T-shirts or, on the rare occasion when they've actually purchased our album, on CD covers. I've even been asked to sign Bibles, but I refused. Then if that's not bad enough, one time this guy walked up to me and pulled up his shirt and invited me to sign his chest! Okay, I've seen Allie sign people's hands and arms, but I'm thinking we have to start drawing the line somewhere.

I guess I never considered this side of the business before. I always thought having a band and doing concerts would be about <u>the music</u>. But now I can see it's a whole lot more, and I have a feeling I don't know the half of it yet. As a result, I've noticed that whenever I start to feel uneasy or intimidated by a particular situation, I slip back into my "tough chick" exterior. I don't like that I'm doing that, but it just feels safer somehow. Hopefully no one has noticed. Allie and Laura haven't mentioned anything yet.

Speaking of Laura, she seems to be handling everything fairly well. Or at least on the outside. Sometimes it's hard to tell exactly how she feels underneath because she's so good at keeping up appearances. If she ever gave up music, she could take up acting. Fortunately, her self-control and smooth restraint makes her pretty cool and dependable on stage, and then when we're done performing she's really warm and friendly with the fans on the sidelines. She comes across as generally well-balanced with her all-around steady-as-she-goes kind of style. I suppose I envy her a little bit too. Naturally she has no idea.

It's kind of funny to consider how different the three of us are. What a trio! And sometimes it just totally amazes me that we ever got together in the first place. How did that happen? Definitely a God-thing.

We recently came up with a little routine that we do before a concert. It's our way to determine who gets to share her testimony. It only took a couple of concerts before we all agreed that it's better not to know when your turn to speak was coming. That way you don't get quite so nervous beforehand.

So, about five minutes before we hit the stage, the three of us huddle together on the sidelines and do the old rock-paper-scissors routine. Naturally, the "winner" gets to speak to the crowd. Not that we think of it as a win-lose type of thing; mostly we just hope that God is in control of the choosing that day.

After the "speaker" is selected, we finish off with a quick prayer. We always pray for the audience, that God will reach out and touch their hearts through our music. And so far so good. Or so it seems. It's hard to know for sure, but the general reaction of our audiences has been quite positive.

As a result of our little elimination game, I've come to think of the three of us in those same terms—rock, paper, and scissors. I see Laura as the rock since she can be so immovable sometimes, but she's also dependable and solid. Allie is the paper because she can be kind of flighty, but at the same time she's flexible, fun and active. I guess that makes me the scissors, which doesn't seem like such a great thing really. But maybe it's because I'm the songwriter and I have to be on the cutting edge—ha. Naturally, I haven't told Allie and Laura about my little metaphor. Somehow I don't think they'd fully appreciate it.

Now, just in case it sounds as if I'm complaining. I'm not. I am thoroughly enjoying our tour. And the scenery's not bad either. Like right now we're driving through some of the most incredible country I've ever seen—amazing mountains and trees and beautiful sunsets. It's been awesome! I feel totally blessed by God, and every single day I'm thankful for all He's done and is doing with our band.

ROCK, PAPER, SCISSORS

three together

fitting in

yet so different

set apart

made by One

who knows all things

knows our weaknesses

and our strengths

hold us close

within Your hand

use us for Your glory

amen

Diary of a Teenage Girl Series

Enter Kim's World

JUST ASK. Kim book one
"Blackmailed" to regain driving privileges, Kim Peterson agrees to anonymously write a teen advice column for her dad's newspaper. No big deal, she thinks, until she sees her friends' heartaches in bold black and white. Suddenly Kim knows she does NOT have all the answers and is forced to turn to the One who does.
ISBN 1-59052-321-0

MEANT TO BE. Kim book two
Hundreds of people pray for the healing of Kim's mother. As her mother improves, Kim's relationship with Matthew develops. Natalie thinks it's wrong for a Christian to date a non-Christian. But Nat's dating life isn't exactly smooth sailing, either. Both girls are praying a lot—and waiting to find out what's meant to be.
ISBN 1-59052-322-9

FALLING UP. Kim book three (Available February 2006)
It's summer, and Kim is overwhelmed by difficult relatives, an unpredictable boyfriend, and a best friend who just discovered she's pregnant. Kim's stress level increases until a breakdown forces her to take a vacation. How will she get through these troubling times without going crazy?
ISBN 1-59052-324-5

THAT WAS THEN.... Kim book four (Available June 2006)
Kim starts her senior year with big faith and big challenges ahead. Her best friend is pregnant and believes it's God's will that she marry the father. But Kim isn't so sure. Then she receives a letter from her birth mom who wants to meet her, which rocks Kim's world. Can her spiritual maturity make a difference in the lives of those around her?
ISBN 1-59052-425-X

Log on to www.DOATG.com

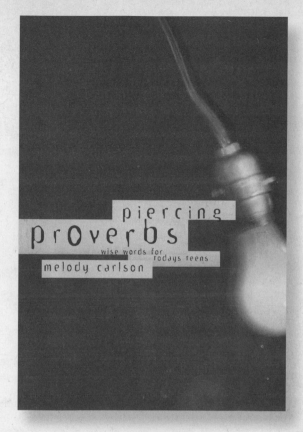

More and more teens find themselves growing up in a world lacking in godly wisdom and direction. In *Piercing Proverbs,* bestselling youth fiction author Melody Carlson offers solid messages of the Bible in a version that can compete with TV, movies, and the Internet for the attention of this vital group in God's kingdom. Choosing life-impacting portions of teen-applicable Proverbs, Carlson paraphrases them into understandable, teen-friendly language and presents them as guidelines for clearly identified areas of life (such as friendship, family, money, and mistakes). Teens will easily read and digest these high-impact passages of the Bible delivered in their own words.

ISBN 1-57673-895-7

truecolors

THINK